I0562945

It is What it Isn't

Stephen Higgins

Published by Chimaera Publications, 2025.

IT IS WHAT IT ISN'T

First edition. March 3, 2025.

Copyright © 2025 Stephen Higgins.

ISBN: 978-1922471475

Written by Stephen Higgins.

Table of Contents

For my parents, Lillian and Larry Higgins

Introduction by Dirk Strasser

Stephen Higgins has come up with the perfect title for this long-awaited collection. *It Is What It Isn't* is both an unsolvable puzzle and an antidote for the banal in literature and life. The title is an offshoot of one of Stephen 's most endearing traits, the ability to cut through triteness and cliche. One of his pet hates is the expression "It is what it is", possibly the most meaningless, self-defeating, vacuous phrase ever uttered, an expression that isn't worth the breath expended on it.

So, what does Stephen do with this phrase? He turns it on its head to show the absurdity of words and cliches that are parroted endlessly. And how apt for a collection of speculative fiction! If there was ever a secret organisation of speculative fiction writers determined to destroy the hegemony of mundane fiction, *It Is What It Isn't* would be their motto.

But even calling what you are about to read a speculative fiction collection is missing the mark. Anything Stephen does creatively can't be pigeon-holed that easily. You'll find short stories, of course, but also the mock (yet somehow also wise) advice of the "So you want to be a" series that ran in the early days of Aurealis magazine. It's filled with his trademark sense of humour, which, as with everything about Stephen, is hard to categorise. You just know it when you simultaneously laugh out loud and come to a deep insight about what he has written.

His example in "So, you want to be a Fantasy Writer" on how to create your fantasy names by using the letters of a single word is gold:

Say we choose the word MARKET. We immediately have a name. Can you spot it? ARKET. It could be the name of the goatherd, but it could also be the name of his village. It could even be the name of his simple but virtuous smithy father, who is a former soldier with a secret past.

Let's see what else we have: KARM—A heroine who is good with horses; TEKRAM (always use the word backwards just in case it "works") Arket's rival goatherd, not necessarily evil, but just easily led; KRAM—a soldier; MAKET—another village; and KRET—another soldier (soldiers account for an awful lot of names in Fantasy).

"But these are all good names," you say. "What about all the Evil Wizards, Dark Overlords and the like?" Simple. You just add a "G" to your letters, or, if you want someone really evil, you add a "Z". You can add both if you really want to hammer home the point. A "G" added to the letters in the word MARKET gives us: GRARK—An evil soldier or perhaps a mythical beast; TEKGAR—An evil wizard, or maybe a city; and RAGTEK—Possibly another evil soldier.

Now if we also add a "Z" we get: ZEMKAR—The evil one! Even more evil? ZGEMKAR! A subtle but important difference.

Stephen's book reviews of SFF classics written as if they had just been published recently are also golden absurdity with kernels of insight:

This new novel by English writer George Orwell sees him going in a new direction: backwards. 1984 is ostensibly set in the future, so, unless I have completely misread the book, it is set in an alternate past. Or it might be set in an alternate future's past. Or it could just be an alternate reality with a dodgy calendar. For quite some time I was worried that the whole thing may have been the victim of a prodigious typographical error, and it was supposed to be 2084, or 2184.

Stephen's idiosyncratic humour runs through everything he does. He certainly enjoys the subtle art of word play. I remember when we were brainstorming names for what became *Aurealis* magazine, one of his suggestions was *The Offing*. His sole reason for putting it up as a suggestion was so that the Contents page could be headed "In The Offing".

So, what about the short stories in this collection? Well, Jim, they're stories, but not as we know them! Stephen knows his speculative fiction tropes and he has the ability to turn them into something else. He has recently hit a rich creative vein, and there are several freshly published and brand-new stories in this collection.

"Black Rock", which appeared in *Aurealis #176*, is a clever and funny SFF insider story that fans of Arthur C Clarke's *2001: A Space Odyssey* will love. The joy of reading it lies as much in the characters as it does in the SFF references. I don't think I've ever come across a science fiction story where one character tells the other to "Get stuffed!". Stephen's acute sense of the trite absurdity in life captures the frustrations of staff meetings with his line *"Erica hated staff meetings as much as the next person, and the next person was Earl who actually claimed he had a medically recognised aversion to them."*

Of the early stories, "The Waiting Tree" is one of my favourites. I'm a sucker for off-world alien-contact tales, and this one has an aura of an eerie classic about it. As with all of Stephen's work there's more to it than meets the eye. In his notes on the story, he references the Australian connection, citing the Boab prison tree used as a holding area for Aboriginal prisoners being transported long distances in the early 1900s.

Stephen has co-edited and co-published *Aurealis* since 1990 (obviously we met at Kindergarten). The magazine has become an institution in Australian SFF, providing a regular professional market for generations of Australian science fiction, fantasy and horror writers. Just to put Stephen's contribution into context, these days we have a team of up to thirty Readers who assess all our short story submissions. In the early years, Stephen did that job entirely on his own. He encouraged and championed a legion of new writers over decades. There would be no *Aurealis* magazine and no Aurealis Awards without Stephen. His writing has always been quintessentially Australian in non-cliched ways, filled with humour and humanity. I've always felt that the people who are self-deprecating are precisely those who shouldn't be ignored. It's time Stephen received more recognition. Turn the page, have a laugh, and see some things you thought you knew in a different way.

Forest/Trees

"Do not think for a minute that I am happy about this," Tier said. "I'm supposed to be on a flight for a meeting."

Alan checked the comp again. There was definitely no power connected to it. He had a thorough rummage around the back of the comp and ensured that there were no leads at all. There wasn't. There weren't even any unplugged leads.

"Nothing," he said.

"There must be something?" Tier replied. "It's still on the screen. Check for wireless or powerpods or something."

Alan sighed. He stood and looked around the room. Tier was by the window, absently looking out as he texted someone. The room was shabby. It had the detritus of misuse scattered about: scraps of paper, an empty cardboard box, an old office chair with one castor missing, and there was the computer and monitor sitting on old table. The monitor had a faint glow emanating from it. In the centre of the screen was the word "Do". There was also a dead bird in one corner of the room. And there was Alan, and Alan had the feeling that this was pretty much the order of priorities as far as Tier was concerned.

As Alan ran a scanner over the walls of the room, Tier was busy issuing instructions to people. The instructions had that perfunctory tone that people used when they were accustomed to having their orders followed. Tier wanted news of another meeting that was taking place somewhere else. He wanted news about an investment he hoped to make. He wanted to change the time of an appointment, and he wanted to know why Alan had dragged him up here. It took a moment for Alan to realise that Tier had put his mobile away and was looking at him expectantly.

"Well?" Tier asked. "It's just a computer screen. Obviously, there must be some source of power to it, and it's been left on. I can't see the problem, and I can't see the reason why you asked me to come here."

Alan wasn't really sure himself. It had just seemed odd. He had come to decommission the nanotech that had been sifted into the plantation. The plantation had started off as an energy source. The trees had been "etched" to provide electricity via the leaves that had been teched into so many solar panels. It was old tech but still useful. Well, still useful until Tier had realised that there was more money to be had from subdividing the land and selling the plots. Alan and Linda Frents had been the only two employees and Linda had left when she saw the way Tier was thinking. Alan had remained to shut down the plantation and sell off as much of the tech as possible. He had binned most of the comp hardware, but there was still this one technological dinosaur left. And now it had a flickering screen with a Word doc open and the word "Do" in a large font. And no apparent power supply.

Alan wondered if now was a good time to mention the ghosts. He thought not.

"There is no power supply to that computer or that monitor," he said. "I've checked and rechecked and there simply isn't. I called you because I thought you might like to see what's going on here before we just left it to be divided up. There's something wrong here."

Tier sighed. He liked Alan. He really did but he could be a pain. He always got into a state about minor problems.

"So, can't there be a sort of remnant of power left in the screen or something like that? I know what you're going to say, but bear with me... All that nanotech up here forming solar panels. Couldn't that have got in here and somehow linked up with the screen?"

"No," Alan said. "It was all inhibited. It had rules applied to it. Boundaries, borders and frames. It couldn't migrate from the plantation out there, to here. To anywhere." But even as he said the words Alan was wondering if maybe that was the explanation. He flicked his scanner wand to nano and it came alive with clicks and pulses wherever he pointed it. The room was alive with tech.

"But it has migrated, I gather," Tier said.

*

They locked the door. Tier drove off to his next appointment, but had promised to send some techs out A.S.A.P., except he had pronounced it *a-sap*, and Alan had thought he meant it as an insult. He left instructions for Alan, which basically amounted to mapping the extent of the nanotech migration from the plantation. Tier also told Alan to tell the techs not to mention anything about it to anyone until they'd determined what was really going on. Tier had interests in lots of tech companies and nearly all of them were involved in the application of nanotech in some form. Funnily enough, Tier knew next to nothing about the tech he dealt with. He used to quip that he knew enough to be dangerous, but his tech staff had privately argued that he knew so little he was dangerous, and that if ignorance were indeed bliss, then Tier was one very happy guy.

Alan could understand why it might be a good idea to keep this to themselves. People were funny about nanotech and they always worried that it could do all sorts of weird stuff. Alan often found people's ignorance about things that were now a part of everyday life amusing, but he put that thought aside as he tried to figure out why this nanotech was doing all sorts of weird stuff. If the prospective buyers found out about the odd goings on, they might not buy the land. Normally this wouldn't have worried Alan overly much, but Tier had given him shares in the company in lieu of severance pay. Hopefully they would have days before anyone from the media showed up.

He put the kettle on and made himself a cup of coffee. It was instant. It would have to do. He walked outside and could still see the dust from Tier's car as it made its way down the hill toward the small town of Trafalgar. He looked at the trees. He looked at the power pole that did not have a line to the workshop. He looked at his coffee. Then he looked at the long line of media cars making their way up the hill. Then he looked at the ghost who was walking near the power pole. He would have spent more time wondering about the ghost, but he really wanted to look at the electric kettle and see if he could get it to make another, stronger coffee without power before the media arrived.

*

"Where are the ghosts?"
    "Why are there ghosts?"
    "When are they visible?"
    "What do the ghosts do?"
Alan was angry at himself for getting flustered when reporters fired this barrage of questions at him and his stupid response had just fired them up even more. Instead of denying any knowledge outright he had asked his own questions back at them.
    "Why do you think there are ghosts?" he had asked, which would have been fine except that, before the reporters could answer he had added, "Who told you about them?" Which simply confirmed, in the reporters" minds, the existence of the Trafalgar Ghosts.

It turned out that one reporter had been exploring a fairly boring story about a real estate developer paying backhanders to a government official to expedite the sale of some land that had been teched up to add to the town's electricity supplies and someone had mentioned the fact that a few people had claimed to have seen ghosts in and around the area in question.

Alan had sought to downplay the ghost story by scoffing at it. Tier wouldn't want the ghost story getting out even if it were patently ridiculous. Unfortunately, he picked the wrong way to downplay it.

"Ghosts are the least of our problems right now," he said regretting it even as he said it.

"Why?" the reporters asked. "What other problems do you have?"

Just then a reporter came out of the workshop. Alan hadn't even seen her go in.

"How come there's nanotech stuff all over the place in here?" she asked as she pointed back within the workshop. "And how come there's no power hooked up, but power's available and why is the word "Do" on a screen in there?"

Why did she have to spout all of that? Alan was confused, angry and a bit out of his depth. Why would a reporter yell all of that out? Why wouldn't she just keep it quiet and ask about it in private instead of telling all of these other reporters about it?

Then he looked at the reporter standing in the doorway and he realised she wasn't a reporter. He had seen her in town. He'd seen her standing in front of signs asking why the town was about to lose their very own electrical supply.

The real reporters all stormed madly into the workshop. When Alan walked in, they were grouped around the computer screen.

"What else does it say?" one asked.

"It just says 'Do," Alan said.

"Do what?" another asked.

"I don't know," Alan said and that threw them all into a frenzy of writing on their pads and phones. "But I'm sure it isn't important," Alan added.

The next day, Alan noticed that the word 'Do' had become the slogan for a running shoe company within the day. It was shorter and more to the point than the slogan their competitor used. Two days later the word went viral on the net as a sort of catch all word for positive behaviour. There were educational programs based on the word 'Do' that were being planned as professional development for administrators just days after the report about the computer screen hit the online news services.

Alan and Tier were back in the workshop along with Tier's senior tech man and his PR person. And there was Dennis Beacham, a reporter who had been elected as the one representative of the media throng that was camped outside of a hastily erected fence. The PR woman was regarding the computer screen with disdain.

"It isn't much to look at, is it? Can we make it do other things?"

"Like what?" Alan asked. "It isn't hooked up to anything, remember? It isn't supposed to be displaying that word. It shouldn't be doing anything."

"Why 'Do' though?" Beacham asked, which was of course what a lot of people were asking. Entire websites had come into existence within weeks of the discovery. There were Facebook pages and 'Do' sites everywhere.

"God knows," Alan said dismissively, and the hitherto unknown Church of Positivism was taking donations and receiving tax breaks in less than twenty-four hours.

Tier had ordered his men to strengthen the enclosure around the worksite and had also organised patrols along its length. There was now a small tent city camped on the side of the hill overlooking Trafalgar. Tier kept telling people not to come and, as Alan had quite rightly predicted, they kept coming. Alan couldn't see why Tier was happy about this. Okay, it got the site some good publicity, but it was a hassle dealing with all of the people.

"It's fantastic Alan," Tier explained. "Property prices are going through the roof. People love this place. Look at the view," he said, pointing out of the small caravan window and only seeing tents.

"Do-town! That's what they call it. And I'm a "can do" kinda guy. People are queuing up to buy land and we haven't even cleared it yet."

Alan's phone had been busy vibrating all morning. He'd stopped answering it simply because he was sick of people asking about the message. That was what it was now, *The* Message. With capital letters. They had also been dealing with requests to see the actual computer screen and people were obsessed with what it might all mean. Alan personally thought it was either a scam orchestrated by Tier in order to improve the prices of the blocks of land he wanted to sell, or it was a weird electronic glitch. Somehow, some power had somehow been stored in the wires and chips of the computers and the screen... And somehow, that power had manifested itself by lighting up a few pixels on an old Word document. Or something like that. Alan was aware that there were a lot of 'somehows' in the whole thing, but he couldn't think of anything else to explain it all. More interesting to him was the appearance of the ghosts.

He had seen them, or had thought he'd seen them, just after the discovery of the word. He was walking up toward the workshop one evening and he saw Kerin Lanley, a reporter, poking around the southern end of the plantation. He called out to her. She just kept walking and then she sort of shimmered, disappeared, and reappeared about three metres away from where Alan was standing. And all of that would have been fine apart from the fact that Kerin was standing beside him at the time.

"Who are you yelling at?" she asked.

"Nothing. No-one," Alan replied. When "Kerin" reappeared Alan noticed that she was wearing different clothes to the Kerin beside him. Then the reappearing Kerin disappeared again. That all seemed so long ago now. Alan had seen ghosts of her again, as well as ghosts of Beacham and Tier. He'd even seen ghosts of himself, which had freaked him out a little at the time. The crowds outside the perimeter of the plantation had grown considerably after the news of the ghosts had got out, but it was all strangely quiet now.

*

The mist just hung in the still air like spores. This all helped to create the thick stillness that enveloped the plantation toward evening. It would get cooler later on, but it was pleasant as Alan walked from the office block containing the monosyllabic screen to his caravan. He saw a line near the power pole that the techs had erected near the van. The pole was draped in solar cells and enhancers and actually shone with the golden light of the misted sunset. It looked totemic. It also looked symbolic, but Alan could not quite figure out what it was symbolic of apart from the obvious. It was only the glowing of the pole that highlighted the slick black protrusion that was within two feet of the base of the pole. Alan didn't know the growth rate of the nanotech installed in the plantation, but he didn't think it should have been that quick.

He walked up to the line and examined it. It wasn't growing visibly, but he was sure he'd seen it pulse or move. In fact, Alan had a vague feeling that the shiny black tech protrusion was aware of his presence. Tier had been less than diligent in recording the types and nature of the nanotech they had used in the plantation. Alan had heard of some nanotechs that had a template for self-preservation. This kind of nano could disguise themselves to avoid detection. Others could emit electrical discharges to discourage investigation by animals. Rats loved nanotech. They had devoured it as soon as they found it until the nano technicians devised a program that they inserted into a lot of nanotech installations. The rats were devoured by the tech. There was some outcry that this was a bit cruel, but by this time nano was a big concern and the companies producing it were able to buy the votes of various political parties. The rats became a part of the system. Some said that there were always rats in the system anyway, so it didn't really matter.

Very gently Alan dug around the black, gelatinous tip of the nanoline that was protruding from the red earth like a finger. He set up a small inhibitor that he had found among the tools provided for him when he had first entered the plantation with a view to dismantling the system. This made him think that the nano system in use was bound to have a self-defensive element. They would not have supplied inhibitors if they didn't think he was going to need them. He stepped back and activated the small plastic circle, checked that it was operating and then went back to his van.

After he'd gone, the nanoline extrusion that had been examining the power pole turned its attention to the inhibitor that Alan had placed around it. All of the mote-like machines within the line began to build and rebuild until they had constructed yet another extension. This extension wavered about some two centimetres above the original black finger-like protrusion, and then it plunged into the inhibitor like a striking snake. The inhibitor and the extension writhed around each other for a moment or two and then sunk into the ground. And there had been no sound at all.

*

Alan watched as Tier's car drove up to the gates. He noted that they didn't automatically open as they should have and was not especially surprised. He walked down to the gate. Alan saw another car pull off the road some way behind Tier's car and he was not overly surprised by that either. Alan reached the entrance just as Tier gave up on his remote and had left his car in order to examine the gate controls manually. He did not look up as Alan approached but kept worrying at the gate controls.

"What the hell is the matter with this thing," he said. Alan assumed it wasn't a question directed to him.

"Well?" Tier said loudly.

"It's probably something to do with the power supply," Alan said. "It'd be a good idea to leave your car out there anyway. I'll grab a ladder, and you can climb over."

"I can climb it, I think," Tier said sardonically. "Anyway, there isn't a power supply. We agreed not to connect in case it upset the screen."

"There is a power supply now," Alan said.

"How do you mean? Have the tech's installed one? It had better be insulated. I don't want anything upsetting that screen."

"I'll show you," Alan said.

The two men made their way up a slight incline towards the plantation offices. The office block was sited within a natural amphitheatre that protected the buildings from the worst of the wind that swept up the valley, but that gave the workers a good view of the valley below.

It was a steep incline in places and Tier was regretting not forcing Alan to bring his car through the gate. He paused a couple of times, ostensibly to look at the view, but he really just wanted to catch his breath. The valley floor was still covered by a morning mist that would soon be burnt off by the sun. And if that didn't happen it would be blown away. Tier could feel the beginnings of a soft breeze at his back as he looked into the mists below.

"What's the problem with bringing a car up here," he asked.

"The problem is you may not get it back down again," Alan said.

"Okay," Tier said. "Problems then. Are they fixable?"

"I don't know."

They started walking again. Alan was guiding them so that they would enter the building area from the side of the car park rather than from the rough road from the gate. Tier saw why as soon as they reached the cleared area.

"What the hell is it?" he asked.

"It *was* my power pole," Alan said. "I'm not sure what it is now."

Tier didn't want to get too close, and Alan didn't invite him to. There was no need anyway. The pole was now a writhing black mass of nanowires some of which were as thick as a man's wrist. The lines glistened as if they had moisture adhering to them. Tier kept thinking of entwined snakes but forced the image from his mind. This was tech stuff, and they had better get a load of techs in to deal with it. He pulled out his phone and Alan quickly slapped it from his hand. Tier shot him a dark look but realised that he must have had a reason. He looked to where his phone had landed. It was already covered by snaking coils of black nanowire. The shape of the phone was still discernible, but that was all.

"Shit."

Both of the men took a step backward.

"That's why it wouldn't have been a good idea to bring your car up," Alan said. "As it is it may not be safe where it is. And we need to move people back further."

"We've moved them back a fair way already. The reporters aren't happy. I don't like reporters who aren't happy. They get all sneaky."

"Yeah, I know. One followed you up," Alan said. "She's just behind those trees over there. I want to make sure she doesn't try to do what you just did, or get her tablet out or something. I don't know what this stuff will do if it gets hold of someone actually using a phone." He pointed back to where the black mass had consumed the phone. There was now only a writhing mass of glistening black nanowire, slowly sinking into the ground.

"It's obscene," Tier said. "Makes me feel a bit sick. They're not supposed to have replicating nanotech up here."

"I know," Alan said. "That's what I was told too. I'm bloody glad I found the screen before I started ripping out the stuff like I was supposed to. God knows what it would have done."

"You talk like it's smart... like it has a defensive capability or something."

"Well, it can acquire or absorb stuff. That much is obvious. I imagine something that can acquire stuff like that would be pretty keen to protect its acquisition."

Tier just nodded. All sorts of things were racing through his mind and the major consideration was getting some tech support to look over the nanotech. It was like no nano he'd seen before.

"Where's that reporter? Are you sure it wasn't a ghost? What the hell is with all that anyway?"

"Over there," Alan said indicating a pile of broken branches that had been heaped at the edge of the plantation. As he spoke Kerin Lanley meekly rose from behind the dead branches and gave the two men a pathetic little wave. She then started to walk toward them, carefully skirting around the area where the nanowire had appeared.

"Can't say I've ever been followed before," Tier said. He was scowling. Kerin stood before the two men and pointed to the mass of wires that made up the pole.

"What the hell is that?" she asked.

"It's a—"

"It's a new type of nano product," Tier interrupted. "It's secret. It has all sorts of patents out on it and also a lot of commercial confidentiality clauses relating to the intellectual property inherent in it. You may not report it, allude to it or seek any further information about it."

"You don't know what it is then," Kerin said. "It's pretty energetic isn't it?" The wires were still writhing around each other. "Where did they come from? What are they doing? Is this something to do with the message on the screen and the ghosts? Do something with these wires? I bet I'm close, aren't I?"

"You do pause to draw breath occasionally, don't you?" Tier asked.

"I need to get a vid of this," Kerin said. Tier grabbed her by the elbow.

"Kerin, isn't it? Kerin Lanley? Please... I don't care that you followed me up here. You know I know your boss. This must remain quiet until my company can figure it out. Now, you're trespassing. I know you think you have a right to tell the world about this, but you don't. I'll ensure that whatever our techs find out about this nano stuff, everyone will be informed."

Kerin looked dubious. "And will we get access to *all* the information you dig up about this stuff *and* the dead screen scroll."

Tier frowned. "Is that what you call it? The message?"

"Someone at the office called it that. The dead screen scrolls. They think it will turn out to be a religious tract or some sort of divinely inspired message."

"It's a bit slow for a divinely inspired message, isn't it?" Alan said. "It's just been one word for days."

"That's another thing," Kerin said. "Can I get access to the screen at all times? If and/or when another word appears I want to know immediately. And can I have exclusive rights to report it?"

"How can you have access to it all the time?" Tier asked. "We can't set up a cam on it. You've seen what happens to tech."

Alan's attention was drawn by a movement over behind the pile of branches. Another Kerin Lanley stood up from branches and waved meekly at him. Then, as she began to walk up behind the first Kerin, she began to dissolve. There was a soft hiss as she seemed to disappear in a slow cascade of dust motes.

"I think we need to do something about the ghosts too," Alan said. As he said it, he noticed a slight change in the glow emanating from the shed. It was somehow brighter.

*

Some technicians and PR people were seated with Alan in the small conference room of a local hall. Tier had promised to rent it out for a few days for an incredible amount of money. There were no others present.

"Ghosts, tech, and message," Tier said. "There has to be money in this somewhere." He looked around at the blank faces. "So, what have got?"

Alan waited but no-one seemed to want to talk so he decided he would.

"The second word has thrown a bit of a spanner into the mix. Everyone was expecting 'Do good' or 'Do unto others', or something like that. 'Do not...' implies a longer message." Alan paused and noticed that all of the PR people were madly making notes, and all of the technicians were looking at him expectantly. He pushed on when the pause got too long to bear.

"Many of the churches that sprung up when we just had the word 'Do' are having to rewrite their scriptures. The Church of Positivism has become the Church of Positive Negativism. People aren't happy. Half those protestors are people who say we are playing around with their spiritual beliefs."

"A longer message would be a good thing, wouldn't it?" Tier asked enthusiastically. "A nice long message will keep interest up. More land sales. Hell, more t-shirt sales too. Pity it sounds sort of negative though. Anyway, we have the message. A little bit negative, but we can work with it. We have the tech aspect. There's no power source for the computer and any tech that gets too close gets... umm..." For once Tier was lost for words.

"Eaten?" Alan suggested.

"No. Too negative. And what with the negative message and everything..."

"How about "subsumed"," a PR person said. Tier looked unenthused.

"Incorporated?" someone else suggested.

"A bit "Trekky" or something," Tier said.

"Enhanced?" Alan offered.

"How is a piece of tech getting eaten by black slithering nanotech 'enhanced' as you call it?" the PR person asked.

"Okay, never mind that. Let's go with enhanced for now," Tier said. "Okay so, that's 'The Message,' the tech angle, and we also have the ghost bit. What's the go with the ghosts? We know that they aren't really ghosts, don't we? That's just a given, isn't it?"

There was silence.

"Wow. You mean they really are ghosts?"

Alan said, "They aren't ghosts in the sense of spirits of people who have died. We are not sure what they are. But they are certainly linked to the tech stuff as they only appear near the source of the tech."

"So, they could be ghosts?" Tier said.

"No," Alan said. "They aren't ghosts."

Tier looked a little deflated. "But that's not been proven one way or the other," he said.

A PR person coughed and gave a little embarrassed look around the table and slowly dissolved into a cloud of dust.

On a trip into town, Tier noticed that the ghosts had begun to turn up further away from the tech up the hill. People, buildings and even trees occasionally dissolved into tiny motes of dust. He got his tech people looking into it just in case there was some money in it somewhere. The dust was found to be nanotech, which pleased Tier as he thought that bestowed some ownership upon his companies. Sometimes it was dead tech and other times motes formed little galaxies and then coalesced into new people, buildings or whatever. There seemed to be no real guiding intelligence behind the creations. Or at least that was the general opinion until the next word appeared on the screen.

The words, 'Do not think,' were now dead centre on the screen.

Tier looked up from the screen in the shed. "When did it appear?" he asked.

"About an hour ago," a technician replied. "We were just doing the routine checks and there it was."

"'Do not think'," Tier said slowly. "No, I don't like the sound of that at all. That's way too negative. It hasn't got out yet has it?"

"Not yet, but it won't be long," Alan said. "You gave that reporter open access remember, and she may have seen the new message before we were able to shut it down."

"Bugger," Tier said. "I hate it when I don't feel I have control."

"And you feel you generally have control of all of this, do you?" Alan asked as he waved his arms around room. "The message, the tech stuff and the ghosts? I mean, we don't even understand it let alone have control of it. Jesus, have a look around you."

There was a pause. Then there was a soft hiss. And the desk in front of Alan began to dissolve. Then the walls of the shed became opaque and finally fell away in clouds of dust motes. Alan began to panic as everything around him shifted and dissolved. He looked at Tier's panic-stricken face and was almost relieved to know that he was not the only one experiencing this phenomenon. Then, without warning, the room and desks all became solid again.

Alan and Tier glanced at each other.

"Did you see that?" Tier asked.

"Yes," Alan said. "Did I disappear?"

"Yes," said Tier. "Did I?"

Alan nodded and said, "It's sort of like everything has been remade in nanotech."

"Everything? You really think that?" Tier said, and Alan noted the fear in his voice.

There was silence between the two men. Alan looked out of the window at the forest. It shimmered and Alan found it hard to actually focus on the individual trees. He turned his attention to the hills and the town beyond and had the same focusing problem. Alan felt some sort of vertigo and realised that this must be how people felt during earthquakes when they lost confidence in the earth.

Alan's reverie was interrupted by Tier.

"So, are we real? I feel real. Do you feel real?"

"I'm not sure how I feel," Alan said. He looked down at the screen with the single word "Do" shimmering faintly.

"Do not think for a minute that I am happy about this," Tier said. "I'm supposed to be on a flight for a meeting."

Alan checked the comp again. There was definitely no power connected to it. He had a thorough rummage around the back of the comp and ensured that there were no leads at all. There wasn't. There weren't even any unplugged leads.

"Nothing," he said.

"There must be something," Tier replied.

Notes on Forest/Trees

This was the first time I had written anything for a specific issue. This one appeared in the 100th issue of Aurealis, and we wanted each of the authors who appeared in issue #1 to reappear in this issue. Sadly, for various reasons, we couldn't get in contact with three of the #1 contributors, and so we decided that each of the three co-editors would have a story in this momentous issue. Both Michael Pryor and Dirk Strasser are prolific writers. The are both professional writers and work accordingly. I, on the other hand.... Not so much. As soon as I started full time teaching, I stopped writing. I had so much reading to do, what with essays and assignments, that I just did not have the time nor the inclination to write anything of my own. Also, I have never been a prolific generator of ideas for stories.

Anyway, the race was on. I had to come up with a story good enough for inclusion in what was going to be a special issue. We were even going to print hard copies of this Issue #100, whereas we had become accustomed to just publishing electronic versions of the mag.

The setting for this one is my hometown of Trafalgar and some of the inspiration for the story is the setting. There are hills behind the town just as in the story. There are pine plantations as well. Who knows? Maybe those trees are not all they seem!

I think I had a bit of a fascination with alternate realities by this stage. I had gone through a period where I was very into Philip K Dick, and I love the way he used to explore different realities in his stories. Nanotech was just becoming a 'thing', and I just sort of pushed these two ideas together.

The title also sees a sort of semi return to one-word titles except I cheated a bit with the slash. I was probably going to call it 'You Can't see the Forest for the Trees' but went for this version instead. I remember having trouble with coming up with something profound to serve as the message on the computer screen. I was very pleased that the ending solved that problem although I do wonder if it is a little too subtle.

Vignette

If you kept your head down and just looked at the grass, you could almost forget that The Store was even there. But the grass would not hold your attention for long. It was not rich and green; it was brown and rough and dry.

The hour approached and I watched the faces of my co-workers looking up reluctantly to see the exact time - all of the big Stores have a clock fixed to the side facing The Lawn. There is always a Lawn. As each face looked up, I thought I detected a slight flinch. It was nothing reportable. It was just as if each person cowered slightly as they dragged themselves to their feet and prepared to return to work. Maybe I flinched as well? I was unaware of it if I did.

As we returned to our places, those who had been relieving us returned to theirs. We would curse them because they would not have done any of our work; but then, we never did any of theirs while they were out to lunch.

The boxes that I had left were still sitting on the floor waiting to be opened and unpacked. The boxes contained greeting cards which I had to count and sort out and then place on the shelves. The cards had to be placed in a certain order: birthday cards, sympathy cards, get well soon cards etc. If the cards had pictures on them, they had to be placed at the front of the shelf. The only pictures that did appear on the front of the cards were photos of The Lawn outside The Store. The Lawn is a large quadrangle that is surrounded by factories and other Stores. There is a tree or two, but it is mostly just grass. The other Stores around The Lawn are all One Product Stores: shoes or food or furniture. Ours is the only Multi Product Store in the area. All of the Stores and Factories are built from the grey brick, so, even though it is a bit dry and barren, The Lawn does stand out.

I settled down to sort the cards out into their various categories. This is a bit harder than it sounds because I had to open each card in order to find out what occasion it was for. The only words that appeared on the front of the cards were "Greetings from North

Central!" Except of course for the sympathy cards. They had "Sympathy from North Central!" I think we should have got rid of the exclamation mark. And, as I said, if there was a picture on the card it was always The Lawn. Although there was one card I found once that had a picture on it that was not The Lawn. A long time ago (I have only been in this Store a short time), I found a card with a picture of a woman on it. She was not wearing The Clothes. Instead, she had a cloth with prints of flowers all over it. It was all very bright and lively and highly illegal of course. Whoever put the card into the box would have been Dismissed if anyone had found out about it. I should have reported it.

I took it home. I stuck the card down the front of the trousers and walked out. I remember shaking like a leaf. Simply by not reporting the find, I could have been dismissed. I guess that I thought that stealing the card could not have attracted a harsher penalty. "In for a penny, in for a pound," as I am told they used to say. I don't know what a penny is, but a pound is like a home for lost dogs, so it can't be good.

I hid the card in my cell. There is a place where the skirting board has come away slightly from the wall. It is behind the bed. I doubt anyone would ever think to look there, or if they did, it would just be through chance. I still get the card out sometimes and just look at it. The woman on the card reminds me of Mary, who is at the same Store as me. I should say that it is just the face of the woman on the card that reminds me of Mary because, obviously, I have never seen Mary in anything but The Clothes.

Most women, and most men, look alike because of The Clothes, but some people have faces that stand out in a crowd. Mary has a face that stands out in a crowd and so does the woman on the card. Of course, it is not a wise thing to do; stand out in a crowd I mean. I know Mary is hoping for a change when she is Adjusted next.

Anyway, that card was the only one that I can recall being different, even though Jim Butler once said that there used to be all sorts of different cards, with all sorts of pictures on them. He said he could remember what they were like. He was Dismissed a while ago. I remember that.

I was working on a new box of cards, and he walked up to me. I should have known something was wrong just by the way he looked. Well, it was just his eyes really. His eyes looked...different. I know now that he was mad. His implant had broken or something. Some people say that there are people who can control their implants. They can sort of turn them off and go on living and just pretend that they are normal. I don't believe that. If your implant is not working, you go mad. And if they can't Adjust it, you get Dismissed. That's life.

Anyway, at first, I thought that Jim was sick. His eyes were darting all over the place, and he seemed scared. He walked up to me, and he looked in the box.

"Cards," he said.

"Yes," I said. "Are you ok?"

He didn't answer me. He picked up a handful of Christmas cards and started slicking through them. "All the same," he said with a sigh.

"Of course they are all the same," I said. "They are all Christmas cards."

Jim picked up another bunch of cards and slowly looked through them. "But they are *all* the same!" he said.

"Yes," I said patiently. "I told you. They are all Christmas cards." I pointed to some other boxes. "Those ones are different. Perhaps you will find what you are looking for in one of those boxes."

That seemed to interest him. "Show me?" he asked plaintively.

I got the impression he didn't believe me. I picked out a birthday card and a wedding card. Both had the picture of The Lawn on the front with the words "Greetings from North Central" underneath. I opened each card and showed each of them to Jim. Inside the birthday card were the words, "Happy Birthday!" written in a very festive style. The wedding card had "Congratulations!!" in the same style, but with two exclamation marks.

Jim conceded that he supposed that these were a bit different, although I could tell that something was still troubling him. "What I think I want to know," and he paused as he collected his thoughts. "Do we have any Christmas cards that are different from other Christmas cards? I'm sure we used to..."

"Not possible," I said quickly. "All Christmas cards have "Merry Christmas!" on them. See?" I held another card up. "In red. Very festive." I realised he didn't want to buy a card. He just mumbled about different cards. I certainly wasn't going to tell him about the different card I had found once in case there was a Leper about.

Actually, I was hoping that there was a leper nearby or even a Manager - anyone who would get Jim away from me. The thought then came to me that Jim might be a Leper himself. They did that sometimes: pretended to be a worker just to see what was going on. They were not well liked. No-one liked to have them hanging around. Hence the name, Leper. It was really just a play on their title which was Loss Prevention Officers - LPOs. Lepos became Lepers. The walked around The Store looking for anything out of the ordinary. They could recommend that you get Adjusted, or even Dismissed. I thought that Jim Butler was a candidate for Adjustment. As I said, his eyes gave him away. Well, his eyes and his obsession with the cards.

Jim really had me worried. I looked around and there were no Lepers around. Typical. There is never one when you want one. I looked back at Jim.

"Why are you doing this to me?" I said. I felt it was a personal thing. I didn't know why he would want to cause me trouble, but someone was bound to report that he had been talking to me for a long time.

Jim just stood and stared at me. It was as if he was trying to talk to me with his eyes. I actually remember thinking that at the time. And of course, that was exactly what he was trying to do. His mind wanted to communicate something, but his implant still had enough control to stop him. I hustled him behind a few of the stacked boxes. "Stop it," I said. "Go away!" He still just looked at me. "What do you want? Why are you picking on me?"

With an obvious effort Jim said, "Because you are different."

"No, no, no, no." I said. "I'm the same as everyone else." I paused as he kept looking at me. "Well not you of course," I said. "I'm not like you." And I wasn't. There was nothing different about me. I don't think I got through to him though. He shuffled off back to the cards. He was mumbling about snow and tinsel. I had to do something. I couldn't work with him around, so I went to look for a Leper. I found one pretty quickly. They always seem to see you if you wander out of your area. The Leper took one look at Jim and then led him away. I never saw him again.

That evening, after we were let out of The Store, I decided to walk back to my cell rather than take The Line. It was one of those still summer evenings with the sun streaking through the narrow slits between The Factories and Stores. The tree on my street looked all the better for the shaft of light that fell on it.

My cell was in a bloc of normal flats, and it was actually quite close to where I used to live. I know that because one of the tenants of the flats told me that he knew me before. Obviously, I didn't have a clue as to who he was, and it was only then that he realised that I had an implant.

After a few weeks he started a bit of a campaign to have me removed to another cell. He said he didn't want criminals living in his block even if they were implanted. The funny thing was, he kicked up such a fuss that the Authorities decided he was Unsafe, and he ended up getting implanted himself. It was only a short-term job, so he will be "out" again, about the same time I am due for Renewal. I must remember to tell him this story so that he will know about it. If I don't tell him before I get renewed, neither of us will know it.

I made my way up to my cell. It was the same as other Cells I had heard about except that, being in a block of normal flats, it had a window. It was barred of course, but I could still see out. My meal had been left, and it was sitting in the tray attached to the door. I heated it up and sat by the window to eat. I like to do that on summer evenings. I was very lucky to have a window. If I stood, I could see a part of The Quad and my Store. I could even see one of The Quad trees. So, it was all very pleasant.

After tea I sat and looked at the card with the woman on it. She was a beautiful woman. I guess she had been dismissed ages ago - as well as the person who took the photo, and the person who printed it. Who else had it? A lot of deaths might be attributed to this woman.

I looked at her face. I tried to imagine it was Mary from my Store. I thought about Jim Butler and Christmas cards, and whether they had been different. I couldn't remember them being different but that did not mean much. I began to think about getting Dismissed. I would get Dismissed one day. The fact that I could even think that meant that the day was not far away. I realised that my implant was losing power because I should have started feeling nauseous because of these thoughts. I hoped my implant would hold out until I got renewed.

The lights came on and I read The Book for a while. Then they went out again and I stood and looked out of the window. I could see the lights of the store and I thought it would probably be a busy night for those on the late shift. There were no other lights...Just a thick, sweaty darkness.

I went to bed. I had a dream. I was lying in bed and next to me was the woman from the card. It was very hot, and I sat up to push back the sheets. This left the woman uncovered. As I looked at her, another person sat up on the other side of the bed. It was the LPO from the store. He looked at me, and then at the woman, and then he drew the sheets back over both himself and the woman. That was it. I hadn't had a dream in ages.

In the morning, I stayed in bed for an extra few minutes and thought about things. This was to be my last day at the store as I was due for adjustment and had to report to Corrections the next day. I thought about adjustment, renewal and dismissal. I knew my thoughts were not right, so I wouldn't have been surprised if they opted for opted for Renewal rather than the Adjustment I was due for. I did not seem to be able to concentrate on things very well. I thought of the woman on the card and the dream I had but I was not able to hold onto my thoughts.

I got the clothes and my breakfast from the tray in the door, and after I had showered and dressed, I ate my breakfast by the window. I decided I would walk to work seeing as how I had enjoyed walking home the night before. Funnily enough, when I reached the tree that I was able to see clearly from my cell, I looked back and I couldn't see the building my cell was in. That struck me as odd.

In my pocket I had the card. I thought that as this was my last day I should return it. I was able to just slip it into one of the boxes so it would be found by someone else. The day passed and I went back to my cell. I was feeling nervy about the adjustment. I felt better about having returned the card with the woman on it. Of course, having returned the card does not alter the fact that I stole it in the first place, but at least now, it is returned. I always felt that somehow, the card was a piece of unfinished business. I guess I was not ready for Adjustment.

*

I started in a new Store today. I work in the card section. Cards and Stationery. I do not foresee any problems. The staff seem friendly. It is easy work, but there is a bit to remember. Fortunately, my Adjustment looked after most of the details. Many of the cards have pictures of The Lawn which is just outside The Store. The Lawn forms a part of The Quad, parts of which I can see from my cell. I did, however, find one card that had a different picture. It was a card with a picture of a woman on it. She is pretty and she is wearing some sort of billowy fabric which is also pretty. It is nothing like The Clothes. The card was taped shut. Inside was a handwritten note.

To my darling Michael,

I know we may never see each other again but remember - I will always love you.

It was signed Mary.

I kept the card. I know I could get Dismissed for that but, I liked to look at it. The woman on the card looks like one of the women at The Store. I like to pretend that she is the woman on the card and that she wrote the message for me.

Notes on Vignette

This story is all a bit "1984" ish. I was heavily influenced by George Orwell's thoughts and ideas, and I had read all of his fiction and many of his essays. So, it isn't really surprising that it all spilled into this little story. It is a bit bleak and down beat, and it would have been nice if some of Orwell's writing abilities had flowed to me along with his thoughts and ideas, but it was not to be. My friend Dirk Strasser and I had just started publishing Aurealis - Science Fiction and Fantasy, and we either needed more stories, or we hit upon the idea that the magazine would provide a neat little way into having our own stories published. Upon reflection I think we needed stories. This appeared in the second issue of Aurealis, and I was thrilled to see my name in print even if it was in a magazine that I co-edited. I have had stories rejected by Aurealis before so it was not a given that I would get a story in the mag just because of who I was.

I quite like the story. I like the structure of it and the way it circles around. I feel it does overdo the downbeat feel, however. I get why the younger me did it, and I was probably hoping to be seen as sort of a mean and moody serious writer. I think I do stuff with a lighter touch better, however. I suppose I could shoehorn some jokes into this one.

By the way, Aurealis #2, where this first appeared, also saw one of the first appearances of world-famous illustrator/author Shaun Tan. He did the cover for us and indeed, he did the covers for a few issues as well as some internal artwork as well. So, I was in very good company.

Cradle

In the broken metallic corridor, there was the faintest soft electronic hum. In the corroded room, filled with dull, dead cryobeds, there was an even fainter hissing. Inside the cryobed on the far left of a group of beds, there was a barely detectable ticking. Inside the mind of the body within the cryobed was an unholy screaming. This produced a slight twitch in a long-still muscle, and this was the first movement that had occurred in the room for a long time. A very long time. The internal screaming then caused a finger to twitch which led to a harness being shifted and a buckle tilted. The cryobed shifted very, very slightly. Air moved, dust swirled and eventually a grain of sand fell against another grain of sand. The process continued until a small hole appeared and once again, starlight fell upon the Generational Starship, *Hope*. The screaming mind was calmed. Impulses were fed into the mind and body. Chemicals began to flow through the lump of matter that was Andrew Lark. Eventually he would awaken, but that process would take a long time.

*

"Ok, so where was it found?" Kith James fondled a small piece of rusted metal as he spoke to his Field officer.

"Outback Australia. Near a place called Shattered Hill. There is nothing there people wise, but there have been some interesting finds in the area. Mostly meteor stuff. Lots of fused iron and the like. Until now nothing out of the ordinary, but lately lots of samples like the one you have. Machined. Made." Lin Hadlee had a habit of speaking in short sharp bursts when she was excited, and she was excited now.

Kith could see the spiral engraved into the round piece of metal that was attached to the small piece of metal. It looked for all the world like an old screw in a piece of metal plate. "It looks like an old screw in a piece of metal plate," Kith said.

"It is," Lin said. "But it is a little more than that. Look at the spiral. Closely."

Kith hated it when field staff knew more about something than he did. It wasn't because he thought it made them seem smarter than him, it was just that he hated people playing games with him even if they were not. He looked closely at the corroded spiral on the exposed piece of the screw. "It goes the wrong way," he said finally.

"No one anywhere has ever put that direction on a screw anytime, anyplace, anywhere," Lin explained hoping the additional "anywhere" would be viewed as a deliberate emphasis.

"Someone must have." Kith looked at it closely again. "I mean it's just a left-hand thread, isn't it?"

"Ok," Lin said, wishing she had not added that extra 'anywhere' for emphasis. "Hardly anyone. And certainly not on a scale like this. We have found tons of these things, and they are all left-handed thread."

"So, we are digging I assume," Kith said.

"Around the clock," Lin said.

*

The tiny hole that the movement of one grain of sand had opened had been widened by rain and erosion. The light from the by now considerable hole, lanced through the dust motes in the chamber. The ship's systems detected the life support levels in Andrew's chamber and a few more switches were snapped open. The systems ran a self-check, noted the fact that there was very little energy available for any further operations, and in a final act, unlocked Andrew's cryobed. Then without ceremony or any fanfare, the systems, which had operated faultlessly for a very, very long time, shut down. There was silence. Then Andrew cleared his throat and said "Nuck." Tech that was supposed to make his muscles supple had worked well, but he was still stiff, and sore. He was weak. He was thirsty. He was hungry. He found he couldn't marshal his thoughts. It was so dark. Night-time? Or is the sky just black? He paused and wondered for a moment. Then he realised his eyes were shut. He opened them slowly then shut them quickly and realised he did not know you could have pain from your eyelids. He said "Nuck" again and discovered that you could also get pain from your tongue and throat when you try to say 'F'. "I'll open my eyes again," he thought, "and I won't move them around. I will just let them see what they can see, and if it hurts too much, I will just shut them and have a bit of think about whatever it is that they see."

He opened one eye slowly. He could see the inside of the cryobed chamber. The glass was all covered in dust and, well more dust. There was however one bright area that was clearly outside of the chamber. It must have been sunlight, Andrew thought. Andrew decided that he would be able to work through the pain. There was clearly a lot to be done. They had arrived, that much was clear. There must have been some sort of catastrophe that had affected the ship's ability to wake them properly. His crewmates depended on him to get out and initiate manual resuscitations. He was actually a bit surprised at how lucid he had suddenly become and decided that the system had hit him with an adrenalin punch. He felt ready for anything. He moved to unbuckle himself and fainted. Sometime later he came to, and that effort caused him to faint again. After the fifth fainting episode he began to despair of ever getting out of the bed, but the thought that he had managed to actually think that much without losing consciousness emboldened him. He opened his eyes and remained conscious. He moved a finger, then his hand and although it was painful, he remained conscious. He lifted his arm and, as hard as he could, which wasn't really very hard at all, he pushed against the cryobed lid. It gave way and he was pretty delighted with himself until he remembered he had not checked the exterior oxygen levels, and he passed out again from the pain engendered by trying to close the lid quickly.

*

The dig area had grown to over ten acres. There was a geometric precision to the patterns being produced by the team which pleased Kith as he hovered above the dig in a company hopper. He could see Lin walking toward the neat set of huts and sheds at the north end of the dig. The hopper put down nearby and Kith brushed himself down as he walked to the sheds. He hoped the aircon was working. Inside was a long table with bits and pieces of rock and small piles of dirt along its length. Lin held out a glass of water for him.

"Water? That's all you have for me?" Kith asked and there was an edge of playfulness about the questions, but Kith actually was hoping for a beer.

"Company rules," Lin said. "No booze on site." Kith sipped the water as Lin introduced an older, slim woman as Peta Waller who had been overseeing the dig. Lin walked up one side of a long trestle table seemingly randomly picking up bits of rock and explaining their relevance. Kith knew a show when he saw one and he let Lin run through her prearranged presentation. He made sure he stood near to where he expected her to produce the 'ah ha' moment. She eventually walked up to near his side, picked up yet another piece of rock and, turning the rock over, said, "...and here you can see the traceries of wires, nanotech and Plasmet that make up what once would have been called a motherboard."

"Ah ha," said Kith.

"It was found about two k's away. We assume there was some sort of crash."

"Wouldn't that have showed up on the satellite shots we got? Some sort of long plough line leading up to resting spot?"

Peta jumped in. "We haven't seen that, so we are guessing that the ship..."

"We are calling it a ship now, are we?" Kith asked. "I'm guessing you have a lot more to show me if we are calling it a ship."

Peta frowned and wondered if she had jumped the gun a little.

"Well, I wouldn't know about that," she said, "but yes, we are calling it a ship. Anyway, we think that rather than a long sliding, grinding impact, the ship... or whatever, smacked down headfirst as it were. Straight in. Hence the distribution of small pieces of wreckage over a large area and the lack of any large pieces of wreckage." Peta indicated the long tables full of bits of rock and metal. "These are just the ordinary samples. We have sent a lot of really well-preserved stuff to the labs."

"So, we have very, very old hardware, embedded in very, very old rock, but... that hardware is pretty sort of up to date. Current as it were. It's the stuff we pretty much use every day... but it's incredibly old." Kith examined the fused rock and hardware closely.

"That's a good summing up of the situation," Lin said.

"Can we have a guestimate about the age of the rock?" Kith asked. He looked at Lin, who looked at Peta. "We have sent samples for accurate testing but thousands of years. At least," she said at last.

*

Andrew awoke again in total darkness. He decided he didn't like this game anymore. Why weren't there lots of techs buzzing about getting everyone resussed? Where were the locals? Surely this must have been a monumental event. A starship from another world arriving. Even if they had been slow to resus, the systems were all preloaded to do the "We come in peace" spiel with associated visuals and music. Andrew had been particularly proud of his involvement in the presentation to the indigenous lifeforms of whatever planet the ship's systems had deemed suitable for the nest egg of humanity. He had chosen the music. Well, some of the music. A song. He chose 'The Loving' by XTC. He was a fan of old music. He would have preferred to use 'Life Begins at the Hop' simply because it was a great little song but 'The Loving' was a bit more 'worthy' and he could see the point of impressing their new friends as much as possible. He did see a part of the presentation before the launch and he was a bit annoyed to find that his song choice had in fact been edited down to a 60 second clip of the song, but that was better going than the 30-minute version of Citizen Kane that had been included. Bureaucrats were bastards.

He pushed open the pod and was a little surprised at the dirt and grime in the pod room. Then he realised why there were no tech staff running around resussing all of the others. There were broken pods everywhere. Everything was dead. Everyone was dead. He stood listening and, with a growing sense of dread, realised that even the ship was dead. Even though he had been cryo'd for years he somehow felt that the reassuring hum of the ships systems had been with him. There was silence. And he felt alone. He understood that he should feel alone while looking at all of the broken, dust encrusted crypts, but he felt unnaturally alone. Primal, profound loneliness. He actually forced himself to stop thinking just so he could accept that fact.

"I am alone. On an alien planet. On my own." He said that aloud just to reassure himself. He did not feel reassured.

He looked around the room. What had happened? Every single cryo chamber was shattered, and each contained only dust and, in some cases, a few desiccated bones. Clearly some of the remains of the crew had been disturbed after death as there were bones scattered all over the place. He shuddered a little. Andrew pushed his way to the door of the chamber and pushed it open with some difficulty. The corridor was as littered with ancient detritus as the chamber. Everything was dirty, and it was obvious that the ship had not been an operating entity for many, many years. But the systems, or at least some of them, must have been working until very recently or he wouldn't be here. He made his way back to his own cryobed. It was still warm from his own occupation. He thought he saw the faintest glint of a faint red LED light, but he really wasn't sure. He felt something he had not felt for ages. There was a breeze. He began walking toward the source of the breeze.

*

Kith weighed a lump of metal in his hand. All of the hardware they had found had been very exciting, but he couldn't see how to proceed with the dig. He needed something to guide him. He had a horrible feeling that this dig could go on for decades, finding all sorts of wondrous things, but not finding that one important element that would keep funding flowing and maintain peoples" interest. He needed answers. He looked up as a technician pushed through the plastic flap of the hut and approached Peta. The technician whispered something to her and gave her a sheet of paper. Peta looked shocked. The technician smiled and nodded.

"News?" Kith asked.

"We've picked up some activity on the dig," Peta said as she handed the sheet to Lin.

"It's a dig. I'm assuming there is always activity. What sort of activity?"

"Movement," said Lin, reading the sheet.

Kith knew from Lin's face that this was something important, so he simply waited for her to supply some detail. "We think we may have found the original ship, or a large piece of the ship. We think it is about two k's away. We think that there is movement there. We don't know why that would be."

"It's only us who know about the finds, and the rocks with tech in them, and all of the stuff in here isn't it?" Kith asked.

"Just us," Lin said. "Well, you know... our company. There would be about sixty or so people who know the details. You said to keep it quiet, so we did." Kith felt that the situation was getting a little out of his control. This worried him mostly because this was the first time he had viewed what was happening as a "situation". Up until now it had been an interesting phenomenon. The up-to-date tech embedded in old rock was clearly a clever prank. He remembered the time some advertising company had ensured sales of a new cologne by shipping it in faux antique Egyptian containers and linking the scent to a cosmetic recipe supposedly found in hieroglyphics. But Lin was taking it all very seriously and so was the technician who had just come in with the message.

"What do you want to do about the movement?" Lin asked.

"Find out who or what it is of course. What's your take on all of this?" he asked Lin. "You've been around some weird digs in the past. What do you make of this?" and he held up a fist sized rock with a wire protruding from it.

"Truthfully? I think it's a stunt. I think we are being conned in some way, but I don't know how, and I don't know why. And I think it's odd that we detected these movements just after you get here. It is a little too neat for mine."

"You think it's a set up? Some sort of con?" Kith asked. Lin shrugged non-committedly. "Oh well," Kith said, "I guess we will find out one way or another. Let's go see what is moving."

*

Andrew was having trouble putting all of the pieces together. There were just too many bare wires, broken conduits and smashed consoles to make any sense of the control panels, but he had detected the faintest of hums from the back of his own cryobed. He had then traced the wires to what seemed to be the remains of a major console. What was left of the screen was useless. There were no speakers. He sat for a moment and reviewed his options. He had determined three possible scenarios whilst he had been exploring the room:

1. The ship had crashed on some uninhabited planet, and he was the sole survivor.
2. The ship had crashed on an uninhabited part of an *inhabited* planet... and he was the sole survivor.
3. The ship had crashed. And he was the sole survivor.

He was still pondering the relevance of that last point given that it didn't really bring anything to the table in terms of action to be taken, but it was all he had so he left it there.

He got up and walked to the corridor. It echoed. He said "Hello?" in a hopeful voice. Nobody replied which was fine by him. Then he realised how stupid he was saying "Hello" when he was on another planet. As he stumbled over bits of equipment and the skeleton of the ship, he began to realise just how thirsty and hungry he was. He said "hello" again a few times, but mostly because he liked the sound of a human voice. As he walked, he caused tiny earthquakes and landslides amongst the broken ship and the landscape that had somehow encrusted it. It had not taken Andrew long to discover that the ship must have crashed and been engulfed by tons of earth... he would have to stop thinking like that... by tons of whatever material made up the surface of this planet. He found he got depressed thinking about Earth and realising that he would never see it again. Or probably any other people from Earth. He cheered himself up by pondering how lucky he must have been to survive the crash, and this depressed him further. He was alone.

That had been one of his things to list. He had started a mental list of the Things He Knew. He knew he had been on a generational starship about to launched toward a new shining future. He knew he had been placed in cryogenic sleep just prior to the launch to save him from the stresses of that launch and to live through the long years of travel. He knew he had been awakened by the ships systems. He knew now that he was the only survivor of what must have been a crash landing.

Whilst he was reasonably happy with the list of Things He Knew; it paled in comparison with his list of Things He Didn't Know which he had given up compiling soon after starting it. He hadn't held out a lot of hope for that list simply because it started with "Where am I?" and was at "Can I survive this?" by question three. He gave up on that list when he wondered where he was going. He reasoned that he should probably try to keep going upwards if only because he had sensed a breeze and he thought that the air from the breeze was fresher than the air within the ship. The breeze had seemed to be coming from above him. At one point he gasped when he saw a large, intact screen on a wall. There had been lots of screens about, but this was the first one that was undamaged. If he was ever going to see any information from the ships computer it would be on a screen like this, so he carefully made his way toward the screen even though he knew there would be nothing to see on it. The ship was quite dead. He just wanted the screen to remain intact for some reason and he moved carefully to make sure it would be safe from any falling rocks he may dislodge. He paused and looked up. He saw stars.

He began a long slow climb up rusted and broken bits of mainframe structure and piles of dust that may have once been office furniture and consoles. As he climbed, he noticed that the stars above were becoming fainter as the sky around them began to glow with the wan first light of whatever sun circled this foreign planet. He also noticed that it was very difficult to tell where the actual ship began and ended. At times he would put his hand on a lump of metal to steady himself, but he also noticed that there was a lot of rock around him. The ship almost seemed to be melded with the rock in places. He thought that the impact of the crash must have caused this, but he was concerned that it all seemed so old. And it was all so still and silent. When he was within ten feet of the top of the hole he had been climbing, he felt an overwhelming urge to say "Hello" again, and he did so, in a very shaky uncertain voice. He nearly fell back into the chamber below him when someone said "Hello" back to him.

*

Andrew was showered, clad in a clean overall, and seated in a pristine room. He had cup of coffee in front of him. Kith and Lin watched him from another room. On the screen, Andrew looked up at the camera and smiled thinly. Then he turned his attention back to the coffee.

"What do you make of him?" Kith asked.

"Well, he doesn't come across as a nutter," Lin said. "Peta thinks he's nice."

"I was hoping for a bit more than "Peta thinks he's nice" to tell you the truth," Kith said sharply. "'Nice' doesn't really cut it as a fully rounded profile of the guy. Do you buy his story?"

"It checks out so far. We've found the ship, and his DNA checks out in the cryovac chamber thing he said he was in. I heard the media are onto it all now."

Kith sighed. "Yeah, they are all over it. But they are holding off on putting anything out cos they, like us, don't know what to make of it all. Funnily enough the government is exactly the same. They are sending someone here."

"Do we know who?" Lin asked.

"Various ministers and their staff I guess."

"Jesus. That could be a cast of thousands."

Kith looked around the makeshift office. "Just make sure they stay off the dig, away from our man, and that they don't get their hands on any artefacts."

"The media or the Government people?" Lin asked.

"Both."

*

Andrew had been found cowering in a sink shaft located in the Gibson desert in Australia. At first his incoherent rambling way of talking meant that he was treated as a sort of found missing person until the authorities could identify him. That proved impossible. Apart from the DNA found in places within the fossilised spaceship, there was no trace of his DNA on any government databanks. He sat now in a small room, with a table, three chairs and a glass of water.

Andrew still had a few things on his mind. His mind did not seem to be able to process much at present and he found himself rattling of the names of things he knew. He viewed this as a sort of rebooting of his brain. He took a sip of water. "Water," he said. "Glass, chair, table, floor, ceiling, two-way mirror, no window, door." He stood and walked over to the door. It was locked. He thought that maybe they were leaving him alone to try to stress him, but he was used to loneliness, and he was used to small spaces. And who were "they" anyway? He remembered being found. Then there was a blank. He vaguely recalled he had collapsed as they dragged him up out of the sink hole, and had come to in an ambulance. He could remember every single second of the trip in the ambulance simply because he was trying to focus on every detail. The people who found him were humans. They were speaking English. In the ambulance Andrew recalled that he kept reading the labels that were attached to everything. He didn't really understand a lot of them, but he recognised the letters and some words. There were drugs and machines and he knew them all. He strove to hear any talking but apart from the occasional blast of radio static there was no talking by anyone. He recalled his list of Things He Didn't Know and he realised that where he was, currently occupied position number one.

"Come on let's have a chat," Kith said. He held the door for Lin and followed her out. Then she held the door for him and followed him into the small room where Andrew sat. He looked sad. Kith and Lin sat opposite Andrew.

"You need to tell us who you are and where you are from, mate," Kith said. "I mean we aren't going to do anything about trespass or anything, but everyone wants to know about this buried ship and frankly, we don't think they are going to be too happy with your explanation." Andrew remained silent. "And the reason they won't be overly happy with your explanation is that it's crap."

Andrew sighed. "I was on a generational starship. There was an enormous asteroid about to impact Earth, my planet. We were the seed of a new civilisation on a new planet. I was placed in cryogenic sleep along with the four hundred others. I awoke here." He paused and looked uncomfortable. "Are you sure this is Earth?" Other inquisitors had told him it was Earth, and he had to admit, it looked pretty Earthy.

"Yeah, pretty sure," Kith said. "Anyway, about your story. I saw that movie too," Kith said. "And if you are adamant about this being true, well, here we are, on Earth, no asteroid, no plans for a big starship, but we do seem to have an old big piece of metal, with lots of technology, embedded in a load of old rock, and I have the world's media coming up with all sorts of dumb ideas and I have government ministers wanting answers. Four of them are actually on their way here because they want to have a look at the ship and at you."

"Who is coming?" Lin asked.

"The Agriculture minister, Paul Street. That Science and Technology guy, George Prin. And what's his name from the Prime Minister's office, John someone..."

"John Sinclair," Lin said.

"Yeah him. And Eric Townes. Christ it will be like the bloody Beatles. John, Paul, George and Eric. The Fab Four."

"What about Ringo?" Andrew asked.

Kith looked a little exasperated. "What?"

"Ringo, you know... The Beatles. John, Paul, George and Ringo."

"No, Eric. Who is Ringo? What is a Ringo?"

"The drummer, you know from The Beatles," Andrew said. "I'm a fan. I thought everyone knew The Beatles."

*

The minister paced the room. "So it isn't alien? *He* isn't alien?"

"It does not appear so, Minister," Kith said.

"Pity. Would have taken the sting out all the crap we are copping prior to the election. But there is still a story there?"

"Oh Yes, Minister," Kith said. "What we have here is a genuine mystery."

"Yeah. People aren't so impressed with mysteries," the minister said. "People like answers not more questions. So, if it isn't first contact, what is it? A time machine maybe? With massive expenditures of power... Incredibly complex technology we can copy... Something like that?"

"Maybe Minister, or of course it could all be an elaborate hoax."

"But I was told it's a space ship. With new technology. That was in the briefing paper. It can't be a hoax. We've flown half the scientists in the country here. Can I talk to the... the person?"

"Just through here, Minister," Kith said. He was enjoying the Minister's discomfort. Even though he was disappointed that there wouldn't be huge technological windfalls from the find, there would be some. The cryotech alone was worthwhile. But he wasn't really sure what he, or anyone else for that matter, was going to do with Andrew Lark.

Andrew stood uncertainly as the Minister entered the room. He knew the man was important because of the way people smiled at him and seemed to be cloyingly attached to him as he walked.

"Mr Lark. It is a pleasure to meet you! I'm John Sinclair. I'm a government minister representing the Prime Minister."

Andrew wondered why the minister spoke so loudly and deliberately. He looked around but there were no cameras, so he wasn't performing for the media.

Kith sidled up to the minister. "He can speak and understand English, Minister. There is no need to alter your own speech to make yourself understood."

"Quite... English eh? You understand English Mr Lark?"

"Yes, Sir," Andrew replied.

The minister frowned and turned to Kith.

"He doesn't have an accent. Shouldn't he have an accent?" When Kith merely shrugged in response, the Minister turned back to Andrew. Once again, he addressed Andrew in a loud and slow manner much as English speakers the world over address people who speak other languages.

"I said you don't have an accent."

Andrew didn't really know what to respond to this and he looked at Kith for help, who again shrugged.

There was then a pause that the Minister could not allow to extend.

"And you claim to have been on a starship that was supposed to leave the Earth to avoid a meteor strike that was going to wipe out all life on Earth..."

After a pause Andrew realised that he was meant to fill the pause that the Minister had left.

"Yes, Sir. I'm not really sure how I go to be here, however. I mean I know the meteor didn't hit us but..."

The minister turned to say something to Kith, but Kith helped up a finger to silence him as another aide handed him a piece of paper. Kith waved the aide away, but the man was insistent and handed Kith a second piece of paper which Kith slid under the first to read later. The Minister kept his peace for a moment before he asked himself who was the Minister in this situation. "He doesn't know?" he asked pointing to Andrew. "He doesn't know how he got here?"

"No, Minister," Kith said. "We didn't know the full truth until just now." He turned to Andrew. "Mr Lark... Andrew. We have ascertained that your ship is quite old. Very old. Really, really old," he added in an attempt to soften the blow.

"It can't be *that* old," Andrew said. "I've seen some of the tech you have and it's pretty much the same. What happened? Did the meteor miss?"

Kith wandered around the room trying to marshal his thoughts. "We don't really know if the meteor hit the planet or if it missed. It may well have hit."

"It can't have," said the Minister, "because... I'm not sure why."

"Andrew as you crawled out of your ship. You would have seen all of the old rock. We have done a cursory survey. You crawled past bits of tech embedded in very old rock."

"Yeeess. I did wonder about that," Andrew said.

"We have dated the rock that parts of your ship are embedded in. It's over sixty-five million years old. About the time of the dinosaurs."

The minister looked puzzled. "So, we are saying that his ship, hit the earth and killed the dinosaurs and so that it was his ship that was the meteor that they were trying to avoid?"

"No," Kith said. "That would be a stupid thing to say." The Minister conceded the point.

"No, what we are saying is that the ship was built, and made ready for launch, but that something stopped that launch, and it is not unreasonable to think it was something to do with the approaching meteor... A splinter of it or a chunk of the main meteor. The Earth was devastated. Your ship was badly damaged, but sections of it continued to function well enough to see it through the millennia until now."

Andrew sat trying to take all of this in. He had been prepared to face the fact that he was alone, but now he seemed to have survived both a cataclysmic event, and an awfully long time asleep. "Ok... Let's say that all of that is true... It doesn't really explain why the earth is still here. If my ship was destroyed by a meteor all that time ago... Why are you still here? Why is everything still untouched? Why is the world unchanged?" Andrew paused for a moment. "And why," he added, "do you guys speak English. I mean I understand every word you guys say. And you understand me. It doesn't make sense."

The Minister thought it was a good question, and he wished he had thought to ask it. He waited for Kith to condescendingly answer it.

"Good question." Kith paused, then added, "It isn't."

"Isn't what?" and "What isn't?" Andrew and the Minister asked respectively, conveniently covering all possible permutations of the question.

"The world isn't unchanged. It isn't untouched. *We* are not *still* here." The Minster was really hoping Andrew would ask to have this clarified and so kept silent.

"Not with you," Andrew said.

"This world is unchanged. *Your* world on the other hand, was obliterated."

Andrew looked around the room as if there would be some hint as to what Kith meant.

The Minister suddenly felt confident enough to throw an idea into the conversation.

"So, we are talking alternate realities here," he opined confidently. Kith looked at him as if he were some sort of specialised idiot.

"No," he said and turned back to Andrew.

"Your ship was ready to launch. The meteor hit. You stayed in your cryobed. The years passed. The millennia passed. Civilisations grew above you and then they fell and were replaced by other civilisations. Until we reached the present. And here you are."

Andrew was silent for a moment. This didn't add up. He knew he was still a bit groggy, but this just wasn't adding up. "So... everything gets destroyed... I am kept alive. And civilisation develops in *exactly* the same way, a *second* time. That's what you are saying?" He let that thought hang in the air for a moment.

"It doesn't make sense," Andrew continued. "Couldn't happen. You are arguing that people, hell even animals... I've seen pictures of birds and stuff on the walls here... All of that. Language! The English Language and what... Every other language on the world? That all evolves in e*xactly* the same way TWICE?"

Kith had an idea. He picked up a laptop. "I get your point. But there is one way to prove this. I assume you recall what your world looked like? The shape of the continents I mean. If the meteor hit there would be wholesale changes to the way the planet looks, at least in the impact area." He logged into maps and looked at the familiar image of the Earth. He spun the laptop around to favour Andrews's viewpoint. "Familiar?" he asked.

Andrew studied it a moment. It was familiar. But it shouldn't have been just 'familiar' it should have been more than just familiar. Some of the shapes of continents were wrong. "It's mostly how I remember it. Some of it anyway... But I could have brain damage from all of my time..."

Kith placed a hand on his shoulder. "It's a lot to take in, but don't worry. You will get over it. The only things you seem to have struck that is different is the shape of the world in places and the fact that the drummer with The Beatles was Eric Townes. It's all a bit nipsy napsy."

"What?"

"Nipsy napsy. A bit back to front in places. A bit odd."

"You mean topsy turvy?" Andrew said.

"What?"

"Topsy turvy. A bit odd. Back to front."

"I'm guessing there might be a few other little differences, but it's only to be expected. But I bet the big things are all the same. Wars, stupid behaviour." Kith looked pointedly at the Minister. "Dumb politicians doing and saying dumb things. Stupid celebrities. An Interweb full of potential and yet full of porn and whacky cat videos."

Everyone was quiet. Andrew was clearly still processing the information and seemed to be about to say something but changed his mind several times. Even Kith seemed to be taking time to accept what he had just said. The minister had also been sitting quietly, but he had a strange look on his face. He was obviously thinking hard, given he was quiet. Kith thought him incapable of speech and thought at the same time.

"This is fantastic," the Minister said at last.

"I agree," Andrew said.

"Fantastic in terms that it is really, really good, not fantastic as in hard to believe," the Minister explained.

"What is fantastic?" Kith asked.

"This. Us. The whole thing. The world was destroyed. The world was remade. Almost exactly the same. It is the single greatest ever argument supporting Intelligent Design. That the earth has a guiding intelligence behind it. We don't exist in a vacuum. There is a God. He watches over us. He created the Earth for us."

"Twice, apparently," Kith said.

The minister was unhearing. "My people are going to love this."

"Your people?" Kith said.

"My voters. My constituents. My supporters," the Minister said. He had a look that demonstrated he was thinking of the kudos that were going to come his way when he made it clear that he was responsible for finding evidence of divine intervention in human affairs. He thought he was like a new Moses, receiving wisdom directly from God himself. Somehow, everybody else in the room who was involved seemed to recede in his sight. They became blurs.

Kith hadn't thought of this. Yes, it was odd... improbable... unbelievable...

"Well, it might argue for something," Kith said. "I'm not sure about intelligence, however. How can a process that simply repeats a history be proof of intelligent design? Sloppy design maybe. Half baked, couldn't be stuffed to do it properly design, maybe... But intelligent design?"

The Minister seemed at a loss for words. Kith felt sure he was about to drop to his knees to pray or something. The room had gone very quiet. Andrew was still examining the map of the world with a sad look in his eyes. Kith looked at the second piece of paper he had just been given with such urgency. It was an enhanced image of the crashed ship site and it incorporated radar or sonar or something. Some way beneath the vaguely recognisable image of Andrew's shattered starship was the image of an almost intact duplicate. A second, older ship.

Notes on Cradle

I remember having the image of a man crawling out of a wrecked spaceship and that was all. This was one of those stories that sort of revealed itself as I went along. As I have mentioned previously, I am not a prolific writer. I rarely, if ever get an idea for a short story that arrives fully formed. They all seem to start with images that then grow into something bigger, and they only grow as I write.

Some of the best advice I got on the craft of writing was that, if you wanted to get ideas, you needed to write. A part of the high school curriculum here in Victoria Australia calls for units on creative writing. I taught English for over twenty years, and I would continually get students who would sit there, gazing off into the distance, when they were meant to be writing a story. They said they were thinking of ideas. I told them that neatly all writers got ideas when they wrote, so the best thing for them to do would be to write, and the ideas would come. They asked me what they should write. I told them to write "I cannot think of anything to write" over and over again. I pointed out that they would soon tire of writing "I cannot think of anything to write" and they would begin to branch out. Even if it just meant they wrote "I can't think of anything to write, and I hate Mr Higgins for making me write this stupid story. Who writes stories anyway? I don't want to write stories. They are dumb. I want to ride a motor bike...." Etc.

Anyway, this is one of those 'grew in the telling' type stories.

It drags in my like of alternate realities, or in this case, alternate Earths. Although of course these ones are 'previous' Earths rather than 'alternate' ones. I liked the conceit of having everything on Earth obliterated and then having it all evolve again in almost exactly the same way. It was just so implausible that it went with the absurd idea that I wanted to get across to the reader. The actual last line just takes this aspect one step further.

Water

The tree was leafless and still and it was so black, it could have been the burnt remains of a tree. Ewan thought that if he touched the branches, they would crumble, like cold coals. No fire, however, could burn for very long in this gully. Apart from the near dead tree there was no vegetation - only water and rock. The water had shaped the rocks, and they had in turn, dictated the course of the river. Neither Ewan nor the tree belonged here. They were both lean and wiry while the rocks were round and solid, and the river surged powerfully. Even where there were deep pools, there was a strength in the water, as if strength was something that could be learned from the rocks.

Ewan had been to this part of the river three times. In the short time that he and Emily had spent in the area, he had exposed more film on the rocks in this gully than he had on their last three holidays combined. He always took a lot of water photos. Water and rocks. He liked their forms. The walls of their home were adorned with images of scalloped granite shapes stained with minerals. Emily always complained about the costs of film and chemicals and paper, but she appreciated the finished results. Ewan told her he was just an old-fashioned photographer, and anyway, if vinyl records could make a comeback, so could film.

He took some more shots, angling his body to get different views. A stone caught his attention. It had a sharp edge which was unusual in this gully. The water blunted everything, so this particular stone must have been broken recently. Kids probably, Ewan thought. They had probably been chucking rocks around all over the place. Or it might have been gold prospectors. There was only one other group of people who frequented the area and Ewan did not like to dwell on that group.

He weighed the stone in his hand as he gazed at the tree. Something was different. There was a shift in the way that the boulders sat or in the course of the rivulets. As he tossed the stone in his hand, a jagged edge tore into his palm and drew a bead of blood. He dipped the stone into the water and watched the blood blend with the current and flow away.

Emily placed cutlery on the table. She was brisk and efficient, and Ewan watched her approvingly as she served the meal. She had poise and was quick in her movements. He believed that it was this poise that had first attracted him. Emily, on the other hand, loved Ewan for his down to earth nature. He saw himself as ordinary, but she viewed him as uncomplicated. She sat and watched him eat with his customary mechanical speed. He was always preoccupied when he returned from taking photographs. To Ewan, the photos were not "taken" until they were developed and printed.

"You will be in the darkroom for a while, I suppose," Emily said.

"A while. Not too long. You don't mind, do you?"

"You know I don't. Did you get some good shots?"

Ewan pushed his plate back and stood. "Won't know till I've done them." He looked down at the plate and glasses. "Don't do these. I'll do them when I've finished. I really won't be long. It's just black and white stuff."

Emily poured herself another drink. "Where did you go today?"

"The Rocks."

"Again?"

"I like it there."

Emily studied him. "You know I don't like you going there alone. It's dangerous."

Ewan picked up some dishes and headed toward the kitchen. "Anywhere is dangerous if you aren't careful."

Emily gathered the remaining glasses and followed him. "Don't try to escape. I thought you were going to do these later?"

Ewan stacked the plates and turned on the tap. "I'm just going to rinse them. I'll wash them later" He took a glass from Emily and held it under the tap. Hot, opaque water surged into the glass and up over the rim, scalding his hand. Instinctively, he raised his hand up out of the water and in doing so, smashed the glass against the tap.

"Jesus! Shit that's hot!"

"Are you ok? Let me see! Emily grabbed his hand and examined it. A shard of glass had sliced a neat, clean cut into his palm. "You should be more careful," she said.

"Yes. Anyway, I told you anywhere could be dangerous." Ewan washed the cut under cold water.

Emily felt uneasy about The Rocks. It wasn't just because of the history of the place. It was just inherently dangerous. "People have died there Ewan," she said.

"People die all over the place. People die in hospitals! Lots of them in fact. If you can't feel safe in an hospital..."

"You know what I mean."

"What! Biddy's ghost?"

"No. It's just dangerous."

"The only danger is carelessness. There are rocks and water there, and the only reason people get hurt is because they are careless, or suicidal."

"That's two reasons", Emily pointed out. "And two dangers as well, now that I think about it."

Ewan smiled. "Ha ha. Look, water can kill you. Rocks can kill you. Local superstitions cannot."

Emily gave in. "Alright, but if you go there again, you tell me. Ok?"

Emily sat and read while Ewan was in the darkroom. She tired of reading and made herself a cup of coffee. As she drank, she began studying the photos that hung on the wall of their lounge room. She moved around the room until she came to the mantelpiece. She saw the stone that Ewan had found that day and she sighed when she noticed the dab of blood on the sharp edge of the stone. She held the stone and looked closely. The blood seemed to have seeped into the stone, dyeing it a watery red. She put her finger to her tongue and then moistened the stone, but the bloody stain remained.

In the soft red glow of the safelight, Ewan focused and enlarged the images of rock and water. Sometimes he enlarged the image to such an extent that it was impossible, on the final print, to tell what was the grain of the granite, and what was the grain of the photographic paper. While waiting for his prints to dry Ewan had looked at some of his other photos from the area. Some he had only taken a few days before his latest trip. The feeling that something was different had persisted. Looking at the older pictures, he knew something was different, but it was hard to tell under the imperfect, red safelight in the darkroom.

Putting aside the old prints, he exposed the frame he had chosen from that day's film The enlarger briefly shone a cone of white light through the cloying red. Ewan took the exposed paper, slid it gently into a developer solution, and slowly rocked the tray back and forth. He repeated the process in the rinse tray and the fixer. As he left the darkroom to wash and dry the print, Ewan switched on the overhead light and the baleful red was replaced by the normal soft glow. He did not notice that the trays of dilute chemicals were still stained red. It was not the uniform red of the safelight, but a filmy viscous red that lay in faint streams, like paint swirled in a glass. The faint, filmy streams briefly formed the outline of a hand before they dispersed.

The Rocks *were* dangerous. People *had* died there. There were myths about the place; stories. There was some vague talk about the place being a significant First Nations place, but Ewan had not heard this confirmed by anyone. There was also some story about a Chinese girl from way back being ostracised by her family and dying at The Rocks. Some young girl called Biddy had also died in the area. Whether by misadventure or suicide was never really decided, but she was found at the base of a waterfall, broken on The Rocks. It was this death that supposedly a catalyst for the suicides that followed over the years. A weird accompanying fact was that many suicides made a hand painting on a rock wall before their death. Sort of leaving their mark on the world in some small way. There was no doubting that the place had a sad feel to it. A disturbed feel even. There were some very ancient rock art in the area famously depicting the hand images that appeared in so many sacred sites and it was thought that this was some sort of inspiration for the hand paintings. All of this, the myths and the suicides were bad enough on their own, but a new story had emerged recently that told of troubled spirits leading others to death. "Misery loves company" was Ewan's sardonic response to this theory.

Ewan walked back into the lounge and placed two photos down on the table in front of Emily. "It has definitely changed," he said. He tapped one of the photographs. "That's the older one. A few days ago." He then pointed to the other image. "That's from today." Emily peered at the two images. "What am I looking at?" she said. "What is wrong with it anyway? It's all grey like it is overexposed or something".

"I'm not sure", Ewan said. "It seemed ok when I rinsed it. The paper might be crook or old or something. It doesn't matter. Look, just here. See this bit? You can see the rocks. This was taken at exactly the same spot as the other one...Only it isn't the same." Emily leaned forward and studied the photo and then compared the two images.

"It must be a different angle or something," she said.

"No, it's not. Definitely not. "

"Ok, well some kids have been up there, playing around with the rocks. Pushing them into the water."

Ewan was not convinced. "Bloody big rocks to go chucking about."

"Well, what do you think happened? Who did it?"

"I don't know," Ewan said. "Not old Biddy anyway, or any other spirits. A landslide maybe? Some rocks might have fallen from up the gully. I don't know. Interesting though. I was thinking I might go and have another look tomorrow.

Emily felt uncomfortable. "Yes, well, whatever it is, you be careful."

Ewan picked his way through the rocks. It was a grey day; clouds hung above the gully and were reflected in the water. The boulders were grey, and they too seemed to be suspended and held in the still pools of water. Ewan stood and stared at the tree. Its bare limbs framed the area he had photographed the previous day. It *was* different. Some of the larger boulders were further to the right of the tree and others were scattered around, but they lay as if they had not been disturbed for ages. There was no damage that Ewan could see. There were no recently chipped or broken rocks, and there was no disturbed ground either in the gully or further up the hill. And yet, it was different. Ewan could feel the change. Despite the clouds it was a warm day and the air in the gully was still and close. Ewan felt crowded and uneasy. A glint caught his eye, and he moved deftly to one of the boulders that he thought had moved. The boulder was granite. It was flecked with small points of brightness where the mineral crystals caught the light.

Ewan watched as the small points of crystalline light formed a faint and unsteady outline of a hand. Slowly, he placed his own hand within the outline formed on the rock. Within himself he felt a small, empty breath of fear. He jumped back and quickly retrieved his camera from its bag. His eyes remained fixed on the outline as if to ensure its continued existence as he fumbled with his camera. He raised the lens and instead of the weak, unsteady outline he saw a fleshy, tanned hand and forearm. He put the camera down and regarded the rock. It just looked like a rock.

"No way, "he said. "No. No way known."

He calmly stood and turned away. Resisting the urge to run, Ewan carefully made his way to the edge of a pool. He heard rocks moving behind him. They ground against each other. Ewan knew the danger of running and he forced himself to keep calm. Cupping his hands, he splashed water onto his face and tried to think of a place to go. To his left was a drop of some four metres. It would normally have been an easy climb, but he no longer trusted the rocks. Directly opposite him was a huge sloping granite slab. He could go there. He would be safe there.

"The rocks are moving," he thought. "Landslide? Earthquake?" The slab opposite would be safe. It was too big to move. As he prepared to jump a small stream, he heard, and felt, the earth shift. The heavy air pulsed and screamed with the tearing of rock and he fell before the boulders reached him.

He regained consciousness. He was scared. He could hear voices. They called out to him. Cold, hard stone surrounded him. A horror at being buried alive was washed away when he realised that there was light and air coming in through a crack in the stone. Ewan suddenly felt the cold of the cavern and dread filled him. He didn't know the voices. He felt all of the dead calling to him. Old voices, broken and hurting. Young, hungry voices. He backed against a wall of stone and fumbled for his pocketknife. Panic drove him to slash at the stone with the small knife. He kicked and beat at the stone until he felt something give. Then another voice called him. It was cold, like the stone. He saw a bony, mis-shapen hand reach for him through the crack in the rock. He heard someone say, "I've got you." He turned and saw another hand reaching for him. He slashed at it wildly with his knife and heard a scream followed by a dull thud. He heard screams and laughter.

As they helped Ewan out, he looked down at the body of the young man who had tried to rescue him. It was broken and twisted. Blood mingled with the water in filmy streamers. Ewan saw some young people, smiling.

Notes on Water

This one was problematical. Between the time that I wrote it, and now, there has been a huge shift in the way that writers use the myths and stories of their country. "Water" was originally based on two myths belonging to the indigenous peoples of two vastly different areas in Australia. One concerned the ghost of a young Koori woman who walked around Wilsons Promontory, near where I live, and the other concerned a sacred place in far north Queensland. So, I was culturally appropriating stories from two distinct groups of native Australians. I was so tone deaf to this sort of thing back then, but then again, I think most of us were.

Anyway, I have changed it and now it is a nice quiet and dark horror story which I don't think appropriates any ideas or themes that are culturally significant to First Australians. I viewed the hand as just a hand. (For those who do not know, there are many sacred sites around Australia that feature rock art paintings of hands.)

I rarely write horror stories, and this is pretty quiet horror. I wanted the feeling of unease, rather than actual fear. I liked the way I worked in references to water here and there, and for those wondering, yes, I once did develop and print my own images. I did it for my work as well actually. I daresay that was where a lot of the feel for this story comes from. The red of the safelight in a darkroom is a very moody bit of lighting.

Universe®

There were thirty- two identical boxes. They were stored in a vault in a bank...behind bars. Armed guards patrolled the vault with the diligence of very well-paid men and women. Each box in the vault contained a small piece of wood. The actual sizes of the various pieces of wood ranged from a mere .02 of a millimetre long to three centimetres. Each piece of wood was reputed to be a piece of the One True Cross. They were all priceless. Even the thirty-one fakes. Milo Benz had just bought them all.

"Never mind how I paid for them," Milo explained to his chief accountant. "The owners are very happy, and I am very happy."

"But you can't just buy something that is priceless," his chief accountant explained back to him. "I mean, they are priceless! You haven't killed the owners, have you? Because if you have..."

"'If I have" ...what? Are you threatening me? What are you going to do? Quit?"

"I just have a professional interest, Mr Benz. I know you wouldn't have had the owners killed. I just don't understand how you could have purchased these supposed religious relics when they are, a) probably fakes, and b) priceless if they are not."

Milo smiled. He enjoyed explaining financial matter to financial experts.

"I haven't really bought them. I've rented them."

"Rented them?" Milo could hear the disdain in Harrison's voice. There was a pause then because Harrison did not want to derail Milo's train of thought too much by explaining the pitfalls of renting bit of wood.

"I have ownership of the relics for one year. I am not allowed to damage them or alter them in any way. I can't even take them out of the vault. Oh, and you are quite right, most of them are fakes. I've checked out the pedigree of twenty-eight of them and they are definitely fake. There are another two that are extremely dodgy."

Harrison coughed a little. He then coughed a little more simply because he didn't really want to say what he was about to say, and he was keen to put off the moment a little longer. He earned an incredible amount of money and that fact was always constantly on his mind whenever he dealt directly with his employer.

"Umm...With all due respect Mr. Benz...isn't it a little...unwise...to spend vast amounts of money...And I am not sure I want to know exactly how much money is involved here...to spend vast quantities of money...*renting* some fake bit of wood?" Harrison paused for a second and coughed again. "If you will pardon my impudence for asking," he concluded.

"You think it unwise?" Benz asked.

Actually, Harrison thought it sheer lunacy, but he settled for a muttered, "A tad unwise, yes sir."

"Harrison, we are talking about a piece of the One True Cross here. You do know what that is don't you?"

"A piece of the cross that Jesus Christ was crucified on," Harrison said. "Allegedly," he added.

Milo frowned. "Allegedly a piece of the One True Cross, or allegedly he was crucified, or existed at all?"

There was another pause. "Both?" Harrison ventured.

"Let's assume it really is a piece of the O.T.C. Do you know how much it would be worth?"

After wondering about the use of O.T.C. Harrison replied, "It is only a *possible* piece of the err, One True Cross, Sir and no, I do not know its worth."

"Neither do I," Benz said.

"But you just paid...You must know how much it is worth."

"I gave them blank cheques. They can write their own price. Oh, and I also bought a medical research centre. That cost eighteen million."

Harrison was vaguely puzzled. It was not so much the astounding news that his employer had probably just given away most of his sizeable fortune, but more the fact that he did not find the purchase of a medical centre surprising at all.

Everyone who met Dr. Eliza Prenit was immediately reminded of their own mother. This caused her no end of frustration as she felt she was always expected to meet impossible standards of behaviour and cooking ability. It also meant that many men were instantly turned off when it came time to cement a relationship in bed. She was then, stunningly attractive, single, deeply mistrustful of men and good at sewing. The Trent Medical Research Institute was her home and hearth. She actually did live there. She channelled her frustrations into her work, a practice that led to the formulation of many ideas that were clearly the product of a frustrated mind.

Eliza had been the driving force behind the ill-fated 'Persona' pill which was designed to alter the personality traits of the user by imperceptible degrees, which would make the personality change seem like a natural development. It failed to capture a market when people believed the rate of change was a little too imperceptible. The patients thought they were being conned. Later research revealed that the first noticeable personality change wrought by the drug was always the introduction of a sceptical, mistrustful nature, leading inexorably to paranoia.

Eliza's other most notable achievement was the introduction of the 'Sober' drug, which was designed to minimise the withdrawal effects from chronic substance abuse. Unfortunately, it was so additive itself, that there were still people in clinics being weaned off the stuff. After this fiasco, Eliza turned her attention to medical hardware in the mistaken belief that messing about with machines would be less fraught with danger than messing about with people's minds. Her first project was a series of cheap prosthetic appliances. A subsidiary company was set up and "Arms for the Poor" began trading. The company stopped trading when it was discovered that, due to a design oversight, all of the high tech, state of the art mechanical legs and arms had the feet and hands at the wrong ends respectively...And in some extreme cases, not respectively.

All of this changed however, with Eliza's invention of the "Replicator". The idea for the machine came to Eliza after a particularly frustrating relationship with a fellow worker broke up when she refused to go and meet the man's widowed father. She felt that the man had a hidden agenda. She threw herself into her work and, in conjunction with her team at Trent Medical, she managed to build a useful medical boon to humanity that did not fall apart or harm its patients. It also had all of its parts in the right places. The Replicator was, to put it simply, a machine that was capable of exactly reproducing and article that was placed within it. The only limiting factor was size. It could not do the big stuff.

Eliza had dreams of medical greatness. She envisaged the replication of vital organs for transplant recipients. She even imagined the day when death itself was finally beaten. How could death triumph when humanity may one day reproduce an individual? The possibilities were limited only by size, human imagination and by the Trent Medical Institute board of management. The president of the Trent Medical Institute board of management was Quintin Guyer, the managing director of the organ trading company "Organs Galore". The secretary of the board was the owner of one of the largest funeral homes in the country. Neither of these two people seemed overly eager to allow Eliza to pursue her dreams of medical revolution. Their objections were based on ethical concerns. Eliza had to be content with using the replicator to reproduce medical hardware. The Board of Management Ethics Committee allowed the use of the machine to reproduce bedpans. Thousands of bedpans. So many bedpans in fact, that they created a glut on the bedpan market. They might have been able to trade out of this problem, but for the fact that each 'Trent' bedpan cost approximately one thousand dollars to produce. After this debacle, the board agreed to let the Replicator be used to reproduce blood products for surgical use and for use in the entertainment industry.

Milo Benz loved walking into a newly acquired property for the first time. He loved to see the faces of officious security guards when they became aware that they person they had just referred to in a derogatory manner did in fact own the building. Naturally, he went out of his way to antagonise any staff he could find on his first visit simply to achieve this result. He was a rich man, but petty. By the time he had reached the administrative block of Trent Medical, he had fired three security guards, a cleaner and two clerks. He was, however, after bigger fish.

"Can I help you?" the receptionist asked. She had noted his silly hat and the fact that he seemed to think he was better than her and had decided she didn't like him.

"I don't need your help, darling," Milo said.

"Don't call me darling," she replied.

"Don't tell me what to do," he said.

"What makes you think you can walk in here as if you own the place?" she said.

"The fact that I own the place." Milo liked this girl. She said all the right things. He decided that if she said that she would rather quit than work for him, he would keep her on.

The girl sighed. It was a sigh she had perfected at the secretarial college she had attended. "Is there anything I can do for you? Or are you just here to play out your delusions of adequacy?"

"You can tell me where I can find Dr Eliza Prenit, and then you can pack your things and get out. You're fired."

"Dr Prenit is in a meeting with the Board of Management. And if you do really own this place, I would rather quit then work for you."

The receptionist sat smiling at Milo in that cold, plastic way that all receptionists learn on their first day at receptionist school.

"Tell you what," Milo said. "You tell me where this meeting is, and I will keep you on and double your salary...Provided you do everything I ask of you. I should add that I mean that in a strictly professional manner. Your duties will not include anything weird or creepy. I have other people for that sort of thing." Milo paused and regarded the look of bemused, but polite contempt that played across the features of the girl. It was the second thing taught at receptionist school.

"Before you make up your mind," Milo said as he searched in his pocket and produced a letter, "please read this." He handed the letter to the girl. She quickly scanned the letter, picking out the salient points - Milo Benz. Lots of money. New owner of Trent Medical. She then made a neat 180 degree turn in attitude. (Day one - So you want to be a Receptionist?)

"Dr Prenit is meeting with the board in room 304, which is just down the corridor, and it is the fourth door on the right. The only members of the board in attendance are Mr Quintin Guyer, body parts trader, and Mr Owen Soph, funeral Director. These gentlemen are, as I am sure you are aware, the President and Secretary of the Board of Management." She reached into a drawer and produced a piece of paper which she offered to Milo. "Mr Guyer likes everything to be on paper. This is the agenda for the meeting, and this," she said as she retrieved another piece of paper, "is a copy of the minutes from the last meeting." She then tilted her head slightly to the right and smiled.

"Thank you," Milo said. "You have been most helpful."

"That is what I am here for."

Milo turned to leave but stopped and turned to face the girl.

"And your name is?"

"Helen Booker, sir."

"And how do you like to be addressed? Helen? Ms Booker?"

"Whatever suits you sir,"

"Right. Well Helen, could you pull out all of the files we have on Dr Prenit, Mr Guyer and Mr Soph."

"Certainly sir."

"I will also require any information we have on Dr Prenit's replicator. I want costs, reports, research, whatever we have. I also want all of Dr Prenit's published material and any references to her or her replicator, from either in house material or from outside sources." He paused and then added, "And as soon as possible."

"Of course, sir. Ah...I was wondering..."

"Problem Helen?"

"I was just wondering where I should send everything, sir."

"Who has the best office in this place?"

"Mr Guyer, sir."

"Ok. Send it there then."

Eliza's meeting with Guyer and Soph had not been going well. She had spent the entire meeting dealing with item 1 on the agenda, which read: "Explore the possibilities of utilising all medical centre equipment, particularly that which may be either under-utilized or applied to a function not fully congruent with the utmost fiscal responsibility and efficiency, in a manner befitting the ongoing viability of the institute and its stated aims."

Guyer attempted to make it more clear for Eliza.

"No, it doesn't say "make more money." Look, just for arguments sake, could the replicator be used for making, say, precious metals? If not, why not."

Eliza's response had caught Guyer and Soph unawares. Her geological arguments left them unsure. Her dissertation on the actions of subatomic particles had them floundering. When Eliza raised the concepts of ethics and good corporate citizenship, they were wrecked on the rocks of ignorance and apathy.

"So, you can't do it," Guyer said.

"Well, not so much can't..."

"Oh wonderful!" Soph said. "You can do it then?"

"No," Eliza said. "I *can* do it, but I won't do it."

Guyer sat back in his chair. He smiled sadly and slowly shook his head from side to side. "Dear oh dear, oh dear," he said, which didn't convey anything meaningful to Eliza.

"Miss Prenit," Guyer began.

"Doctor Prenit," Eliza corrected.

"*Doctor* Prenit," Guyer continued. "Do you know how much money this establishment needs just to fund your own research?"

"No," Eliza said.

"Lots," Guyer said.

Eliza thought for a moment. "That much? I had no idea."

Soph took up the argument. "So, you can see why we think it would be a good idea if we put the Replicator of yours to um, better use. You see, if you replicated some gold, for instance, that would free up our financial constraints."

"Our very tight financial constraints," Guyer added.

"Indeed, the very tight financial constraints - Thank you Mr Guyer- that we find ourselves in." Soph paused, but the look on Eliza's face made him think that more was needed. "Thereby freeing up the time and money and effort required simply to keep this establishment running," Soph sat back. There was a pause and this time Guyer thought that maybe a bit more was needed.

"And of course that means that considerably more time and effort can be dedicated to your wonderful work in the medical field," Guyer concluded.

Eliza liked Guyer and Soph. They didn't see her as a mother figure for a start. They saw her as an asset. An under-utilized asset certainly, or at least that was how they viewed the Replicator. In the minds of Guyer and Soph, Eliza and the replicator were inextricably entwined. For a start she was the only one who knew how to program the machine. She had trained others to operate the replicator, but every one of the trainees had started trying to replicate jewellery and other valuables and Eliza had sacked them on ethical grounds. Guyer and Soph had thought that these people had demonstrated initiative, and they kept on sending in new trainees with strict instructions to learn the secrets of the machine, and to replicate valuables. Both Guyer and Soph knew of the rumours about Trent Medical being sold and they both wanted to obtain the secrets of the replicator before it was taken from them. Failing that, they wanted a ton of replicated gold and jewels.

Milo Benz stood outside the door listening intently to the conversation via a bug he had ordered installed into every room in the Institute some weeks before. Helen had provided a chair and a cup of coffee. Milo had finished his coffee, and he was now a little bored, so he decided to make his entrance. Eliza saw Milo enter. Eliza didn't recognise him as staff, and she assumed that he must have been lost.

"Can I help you?" she asked.

"Yes," said Milo.

*

They stood in the vault. Most of the boxes had been cleared and stacked into a corner. On a small table in the centre of the room were two boxes. Eliza walked to the table and picked up a box. It was small and light and as soon as she touched it, alarms sounded. Lights flashed and strobed and men with guns bounded into the room. Milo flicked a switch.

"Sorry, I forgot to disarm the alarm," Milo turned to the men with guns. "There is no problem. Sorry, my fault. Well done though.

You were very quick." He turned back to Eliza and indicated the box that she had dropped when the alarms sounded.

"Please, feel free."

Eliza hesitantly picked up the box again. She unclipped the lid, unfastened the binding, and then held the box out to Milo so he could tap in the access code that was now required. Then she unlocked the box with the tiny key that Milo gave her. This revealed another small box with some string tied around it. The knot was particularly hard to undo but eventually Eliza managed it. She lifted the lid of the box. There was a small piece of wood inside the box. It was bathed in an unearthly golden glow. Milo stood at her shoulder.

"Impressive isn't it?" he said. "The switch for the light is on the side." Eliza located the small switch, and the glow disappeared.

"What do you think?" Milo asked.

"It's just a piece of wood," Eliza said. "There shouldn't be any problems."

"And you don't have any ethical problems about replicating this particular piece of wood?"

"No. Should I?"

"That's not for me to say," Milo said. "A lot of people might find it unethical to replicate a piece of The One True Cross. You are not a believer I take it Dr Prenit?"

"I am one of those boring people who believes in something, but I don't really know what it is, and I guess God is as good a word for it as any other."

"So, you will replicate this piece of wood?"

"The deal is, I replicate the wood, and then I am free to turn my attention to medicine. I can replicate anything I want."

Milo nodded. "Anything you want...remembering of course that every time you replicate something, you also replicate a piece of this wood. We will keep the original safe after you have replicated it once. So just bung in a replicated bit of wood with whatever you are replicating."

"You do know that you do not need to keep the original safe," Eliza said. "Once it is replicated, then both are still the originals, there is no difference whatsoever."

"Humour me," Milo said. "So, you can keep producing whatever you like, as long as you keep producing my bits of wood. Or you can dedicate the machine to doing wood for x amount of time and then have that same amount of time to do your own thing. We can work on the details. Either way, you get your work done, and I get lots of replications. Deal?"

Eliza frowned. "What will you do with all of these bits of wood?"

"I'll sell them Dr Prenit."

Eliza was a little taken aback. "I actually expected you to say, "Everyone deserves a piece of The One True Cross. No one person should have access to a religious relic of this importance..." Something like that anyway."

Milo shrugged. "I'm an honest man. If some religious bible bashers get some pleasure out of all this then fine, but I'm in it for the money."

"One thing has always intrigued me Mr Benz..."

"Mm? What's that?"

"Well, you are already very rich...Why is it that very rich people always seem intent on increasing their wealth? You people never seem to sit back and enjoy your money. Is it a power thing? Money brings power and you want more and more power?"

Milo thought for a moment. No-one had ever asked him this question before. "I think it might be that for a lot of people," he said. "I mean, power is addictive...But no. The reason I keep trying to increase my wealth is...I want to see how much I can get. It's sort of a hobby."

Eliza was impressed with his honesty and by the fact that he had not said she reminded him of someone. "How did you find out about the Replicator?" she asked. "You don't strike me as the type who reads medical science journals."

"That was just a piece of luck. I own a bedpan manufacturing company. Well. They make other stuff too but specialize in bedpans. I have to admit that I don't keep a very close tab on this particular venture, but one day I was having a peek at the numbers and discovered the stock had plummeted. Everyone was buying these new-fangled bedpans from Trent Medical, and very expensive bedpans they were too."

Eliza was getting a lesson in business ethics. Soph and Guyer had told her that the replicated bedpans had not sold well. "Too expensive," they had said. "Not cost efficient. Wrong colour."

Milo paused and regarded Eliza's face. "I daresay Soph and Guyer told you sales were poor."

Eliza nodded.

"Nah, sold like hotcakes. Everyone heard that they were high tech products, and the price tag meant that they must have been good. So, everyone bought them. Then there was a glut on the market, and everyone got out of bedpans. I bet Soph and Guyer had tried to get you replicating money or jewels."

Eliza nodded again. Milo smiled ruefully and picked up the box containing the relic. "It always amuses me...The little ruses that little men perpetuate to make more money. No one thinks big anymore. Look at all of these boxes." Milo swept his arms towards the stack of boxes placed neatly in a corner of the room. "All of these fakes are the result of little men trying to make a little bit of money. These people knew or at least suspected that they owned fakes. Yet they were still prepared to make me pay for them."

Eliza looked at the boxes. "How much did they charge you?"

"I don't know."

"Sorry?"

Milo started to examine the small piece of wood held in the box he had picked up. "I don't know. I gave the owners a blank cheque. They can write their own amount." He noted the look on Eliza's face. "You probably think I am made of money...Or mad. My accountant would agree with you by the way."

"Both thoughts had crossed my mind," Eliza said.

"You would be surprised how little imagination these people have. They will all be agonising about how much they should charge." Benz adopted a fearful tone. "If I charge too much, Benz will make my life a misery. He's rich. He could do that. But if I charge too little, he will think I am a fool and I will be cheating myself." Little people, little thoughts. That's what Guyer and Soph are like."

"And what are you like?" Eliza asked.

"Oh, I'm just like everyone else. I have all of the little foibles and traits that make everyone lovable or horrible. I just have an awful lot of money and so those foibles and traits get amplified." He held the box open for Eliza. "I've forgotten, did you agree to replicate this?"

"Yes."

"Oh good."

"It will take about two months."

"That long?"

"Wood's tricky."

*

The Replicator was installed in the vault. The guards were increased in both number and size. Eliza had a bed and cooking facilities set up in the vault, although she still spent a lot of time at the Medical Centre. Milo had thoughtfully provided bathroom facilities thinking that Eliza intended to move in with the replicator, but she assured him that the bed was only for the programming stage. She just thought it would be easier to get the work done if she didn't have to go home every night.

Milo believed in the notion of mad scientists and was keen to accommodate Eliza's every wish, no matter how loony he thought it or she, was. He had been surprised at how easily she had been manipulated, by Guyer and Soph but also by himself. He had not had to resort to threats of firing her or violence. He was quite prepared to engage in violence if the occasion required it, but he preferred to simply manipulate people where possible. He did not like Eliza. She reminded him of his mother. But, he reasoned, you didn't have to like people to use them up and discard them. He walked around the replicator and felt a vague dissatisfaction that there were no banks of lights and strings of cable all over the place. The Replicator was just a grey box, two metres long, one metre wide, and one metre deep. On the top of the box were two small lights: one red and one green. There were small glass viewing holes on the side. There was a usb outlet and Eliza's laptop was currently plugged into that. And there was a plug on a long lead. That was it.

Milo looked up as Eliza wheeled another machine into the vault. This one looked more promising. It had a screen and rows of promising lights. It also had dials and little vu meters.

"Is that part of the replicator?" he asked.

"No. This is a particle analyser. I have to identify all of the components of the item to be replicated."

Milo looked dubious. "It's wood. You don't need a machine to tell you that."

"True. But I do need a machine to tell me what type of wood it is. I need a complete rundown of everything that makes it a piece of wood. Then I can provide the replicator with all of the necessary component particles to make a copy."

Milo thought about this for a second. "Are you saying...that in order to make a copy ... you have to make a copy?"

"Not quite. But I do need to provide it with material. It can't make something out of nothing."

"Ok, well whatever you need, just yell out. Although I suppose to replicate a piece of wood, all you are going to need is another piece of wood. Right?"

"Yes,"

"I could have saved myself a lot of money here, couldn't I? I could have just got any old piece of wood and called it a piece of the One True Cross."

"Yes. And that is what they did," Eliza said indicating the boxes of fakes. "That is what the little people would do. You on the other hand will own a replicant of the One True Cross. It will be as real as the original. Identical in every respect. The replicator needs the building blocks of the thing being replicated. If I were replicating a diamond, I could use carbon, but it would take longer. But if I used a real diamond, maybe inferior in quality when compared to the diamond being replicated, then the replication is quicker, as the basic building blocks are there."

"Ok...I get it. As long as the replicated thing is identical, I'll be happy." Milo said.

*

Milo Benz was in the middle of a meeting when he received news that Dr Prenit wanted to speak to him. Milo closed the meeting and picked up the phone.

"Dr Prenit," he said, never really knowing if he should use her title or not. "What can I do for you?"

Eliza told Milo what she had discovered and suggested that Milo should pop around to the vault. Milo was out of his office and on his way before they had concluded the conversation.

"Blood?" Milo asked as he walked into the vault. "Are you sure?"

Eliza pulled a sheet of figures from the analyser and showed them to Milo. "These figures represent the wood and are expected," she said. "Decayed carbohydrates, carbon etc. However, these little glitches in the pattern mean the presence of other organic materials. I ran a system comparison and came up with particles consistent with blood products. There are some other micros in there. Sweat maybe? Skin?"

Milo looked at the small piece of wood with something approaching awe. "So, what you are saying is.... This piece of wood contains.... *His* blood?"

"No," Eliza said. "What I am saying is that this piece of wood has got some blood on it. It could belong to any number of people. I mean, how many people could have handled this in two thousand years?"

Milo thought about this for a moment. "Actually, probably not that many if you think about it. If this is a piece of The Cross, people would have treated it with the utmost reverence down through the ages. Not many people, if any, would have been allowed to touch it, let alone bleed all over it." Milo paused again in wonder. "You know what this means?"

"Lots more money," Eliza said sardonically. "Amongst other things," she added, giving Milo the benefit of the doubt.

"What other things?" Milo asked, suddenly excited by the possibility of things he had not thought of.

"Oh I was just thinking of, you know...Proof of Christ" s existence? Questions of faith and belief. Life after death. Those sorts of things."

"Oh ok. Yeah, right that stuff. Listen, we can replicate this blood, can't we? You used to replicate blood for the Trent Centre."

"I can replicate it, yes. But it isn't blood, Mr Benz. It is merely particles of matter found in blood."

"Don't you worry yourself about all that detail Doctor. We can leave that sort of thing to my marketing people. What I want you to do is to start replicating this stuff right away. How long is it going to take to get up and running on this? We can sort of put the wood thing on the back burner."

Eliza thought for a moment. "Well, we still have a lot of idents to do. I think the first replications will be in about six to eight months."

"That long? The wood was only going to take two months. The blood is going to hold us back another six months?"

"Yes," Eliza said.

*

In the eight months that followed, word leaked out about the project. Religious groups picketed the building that housed the vault. They argued that it was blasphemous to apply commercial laws to religious practice. This only came about because Milo applied for a patent on the blood of Christ. On the days that various religious groups were not in attendance, other groups protested that the whole thing was a scam. Evangelical Christians threatened to blow up the building, as did, oddly, various atheist groups. The religious world was in uproar. Any qualms that Milo might have had about the profitability of the project were erased when advance orders for replicated fragments of the Cross exceeded two billion dollars. The religious extremists had failed to win over that huge mass of the middle ground who wanted their spiritual life to have a merchandising concession just like everything else. Milo's plans to cut up the replicated wooden pieces into even smaller pieces were quashed by his advisors when they learned he planned to name the slivers of wood, "Toothpicks". It was probably good that they did not learn of his plan to call the larger pieces, "Whoppers". Even so, Milo knew that the potential profits would exceed his wildest dreams, and Milo had some very wild dreams indeed.

The day that the replication was due to be completed was known to only a select few: Milo, Eliza, two guards, and the world's media. Milo fought his way through the crowds and finally gained the door. Once inside the building he walked quickly and confidently toward the vault, resisting the urge to run. Eliza had informed him that the replication was nearing completion, and he wanted to be there when she opened the replicator. He tried to convince himself that there would be nothing very special about what he would see, and it was likely he would simply see two small amounts of blood or maybe piles of dusty blood constituents. He wasn't sure. He had insisted on using his own blood as a basis for the replication. And he had provided bits of wood from his own garden. He regretted not asking more questions for some reason.

He entered the vault, and his eyes were drawn to the grey box softly humming in the centre of the room. The green light was glowing, indicating that the program had run its course. He then looked expectantly at Eliza, and then at one of the guards. They seemed edgy, unsure.

"Did it work ok?"

"Umm.... Milo...Mr Benz... We have a small problem," Eliza said.

"Okay. Small problems I can cope with. What is it? Is the wood ok? We haven't lost the wood have we?"

"The wood is definitely in the replicator, Mr Benz." Eliza said.

"Milo, please. Both bits of wood? So, the blood is in there too? The replication worked?"

Eliza drew a deep breath and collected her thoughts. This process took some time as her thoughts had been scattered pretty widely when the Replicator had finished the program, and she had seen what was in the box.

"I can state confidently," Eliza stated with no trace of confidence that Milo could discern, "that everything we put into the Replicator is still in the Replicator."

"Ok," said Milo. "So the small problem is...?"

"Umm. The small problem is not that small really." Eliza paused again. "If I can explain..."

"I was just asking myself the same question," Milo said.

"We have the original fragment. It is here in the originator compartment. See?"

Milo looked and nodded. "And the replicated fragment?" he asked

"That is in the main compartment. The problem is, I don't know exactly where in the main compartment."

Eliza smiled nervously. The guard looked at a speck of something on the wall with a level of interest that showed how much he did not want to get involved in the conversation. Milo was getting frustrated.

"Doctor, I am getting bad information. I am getting evasions and half-truths." He pointed at the far end of the box. "That is the main compartment. Yes?"

Eliza nodded.

"The replicated fragment of wood, with its bit of blood, is in there. In that compartment, yes?"

"Almost certainly," Eliza said.

"So, what the hell is the problem? Is it invisible or something?"

"I'm not sure how to explain this," Eliza said.

"That much, I'm getting," Milo yelled. He calmed himself. "Do, please try."

"When the program finished, I ran a standard particle analysis, just to be sure that the replication was complete and whole. If you open the replicator too early you get errant particles contaminating the replication. And the little green light has been known to be unreliable."

"Jesus!" Milo exclaimed. "I'm so glad we are sticking to high tech equipment for this multi-billion-dollar operation. Go on."

"Well, the results I got were a little disconcerting, so I checked it all out with a mass analyser, and some imaging software. And I still wasn't happy, so I got a laser range finder and a Werner Ray generator..."

"And?"

"And finally, I had a look in the little window on the side of the box. Take a peek."

Milo looked thoughtfully at Eliza, wondering if this was some sort of prank. He looked at the guard who was still fascinated with a part of the wall. He then crouched to the level of the small window on the side of the Replicator. He saw a star field. A big one. Sharp, clear clusters of stars swirled and billowed as far as the eye could see. There were nebulae and planets. Dust clouds and comets. The stars drew the eye further into the field where there were blue giants and red dwarf stars scattered like jewels."

"Oh. My. God," Milo said.

"Quite possibly," Eliza replied. "I haven't been able to measure it yet. All the readings go off the charts like there was an infinite space in there."

"What is it? How did it get in there?"

"I don't know," Eliza said. "That's the answer to both of your questions. It seems to be a universe. I don't know if it is a replica of ours or an alternate one. I think it must be a replication though. God knows how it got there." She paused and thought about what she had just said. "I didn't mean to sound facetious," she said.

Milo straightened up with some effort. It was difficult to tear oneself away from the window. "So, you think that is a replication of our universe?"

"I can't think of another explanation," Eliza said.

"Have you opened it? The box I mean."

"No! How do we know what would happen?" Both Eliza and Milo stood in silence, gazing at the grey box. At the mention of opening the box, the guard had moved slightly loser to the door.

"Do you know what this means?" Milo asked Eliza.

"No. Do you?"

"Not really," Milo said. "I think we need help. Any ideas?"

Eliza thought for a moment. "Well, we need experts...Physicists. Astronomers... I don't know. Philosophers? Theologians? Poets maybe. Who knows?"

"Poets? Seriously?" Milo asked.

"They are going to have as much idea as anyone else. Anyway, don't poets think about big ideas like life, and religion and everything?" Eliza's knowledge of poetry was firmly rooted in the Romantic period of Wordsworth and Shelley. She had studied them at school and had been left with the belief that, if you wanted an interpretation of some unknown or unknowable thing, you sought out a poet. She had dated many of them. She had then consulted many others and heard their thoughts about life, love, courtship and the value of sex, especially with poets.

The experts were duly called in. The astronomers believed the universe within the replicator to be an exact copy of our own. They wanted to study it as I provided a unique perspective of the stars. The physicists declared the whole thing was impossible and it was probably a hoax. The philosophers agreed that it was impossible but then shrugged and then wondered who decided what was or was not possible. They went off to a side room to argue the point. The theologians were torn between worshipping the box and containing their joy at being proved right...Even though they didn't know *how* they were right. They also agonised over what this was going to do to the idea of faith as the bedrock of Christian belief. But then they thought of the full churches and looked forward to a golden age of Christianity. The poets applied for grants from the government and tried to have sex with the astronomers.

After a few days, Milo decided they were not going to get an answer. "I vote open the box," he said. He looked around the room. There were still a few theologians and philosophers hanging around as well as a happy looking poet and some astronomers. Everyone just looked at everyone else. Milo was tired of procrastination and just wanted someone to make a decision. He also reasoned that as he owned the Replicator and still had some rent time on the fragment from the Cross, he should be the one who made the decision.

"Has anyone else got a vote," Eliza asked.

"No, but if anyone has any meaningful arguments to make, I will listen to them. As long as it isn't just "We don't know what will happen." I'm over that argument." He paused. "Well? Anyone?"

The room was quiet for a while until an old Bishop from a local diocese spoke. "I believe in a loving God," he said. "I do not think He would have placed this wonder into our hands if He did not wish us to examine it further."

"Wonderful," Milo said with some feeling.

"But I might be wrong," the Bishop added meekly. "It might be a temptation."

"Like the apple from the tree of knowledge?" Eliza asked.

"Something like that, yes," the Bishop said, but he didn't sound sure.

"Well, I am going to open it. So it will be me that gets turned into a pillar of salt or whatever," Milo said, hoping to display his knowledge of biblical references. "I suggest anyone who thinks this will be dangerous should leave the room."

Everyone, except Eliza, calmly walked out of the room. Someone shut the door, adding another blow to Milo's confidence.

"You are not going to leave?" he said to Eliza who shook her head. "Thank you for that. Your confidence means a lot to me." Milo placed his hands on the lid of the box.

Eliza looked at him pointedly. "I just think that, if it is going to be dangerous, simply leaving the room is not going to be far enough away."

"Oh. Ok," Milo said. "Ready?"

"No. But it you are waiting for me to be ready, we will be here a long time."

"Ok," Milo said. "Here we go."

Milo lifted the lid.

For a fraction of a second there was nothing. Then, there was a bang. A big bang. The sort of bang you get when you smash an inflated paper bag against the palm of your hand...and the paper bag is as big as a universe, and so is your hand. It was the sound of universes colliding. Just before they were totally obliterated, both Milo and Eliza thought they heard the sound of horsemen. Eight of them.

*

There was nothing. A vast, great inconceivable nothingness...except for a grey box that was floating in the nothingness. A small green light on the top of the box suddenly flicked on.

Notes on Universe®.

I remember this one being a lot of fun to write. I have always had an interest in science fiction that explores religious beliefs, and I guess that explains a lot of what is going on here. I am not a particularly religious person. I was raised a catholic and that always seemed to be a reliable way to turn people off religion. I think I have made my criticisms of organised religion fairly plain in a few stories, but I think this is more a criticism of greed than it is of religion. Some might argue that the two concepts are linked.

I think I saw very early on that there was a connection between religious beliefs and science fiction. I was very into super hero comics as a child and I quickly realised that the major characters of religious stories were not unlike modern super heroes.

Originally, the character called Milo Benz, was named Mika Tenz. This name must have appealed to me as I have used the same name in other works of fiction. It was pretty much the same character. Anyway, I thought it best to change it.

There was also one other small change that I made to the original. The original version finished on a very dark note. The last line of the original version was, "But then it flicked off again." So mentally you can use that version if you want.

The Waiting Tree

Waters tapped a stick against the polished leather of his boot. It was an impatient, incessant action. He gradually became aware that the group of natives being addressed by Lieutenant Fleck seemed to have become mesmerised by the dull beat of the wood on the leather. Fleck's halting dissertation had long since lost its audience. Waters slapped his calf with finality and strode toward the group.

"Is there a problem Fleck?

The lieutenant turned, his hands still in mid gesture.

"I seem to be having a little trouble understanding them sir. "The..." Fleck paused as he struggled to find the right word. "The idiom is a variation of that commonly used by the people that we encountered earlier...Sir."

Waters smiled. He almost liked Fleck. The man had a disposition that made it difficult to dislike him. It was this trait that stopped Waters from actually liking him. He was too amiable.

"Perhaps if you paid more regard to their understanding us, Fleck, as opposed to you understanding them. Do they understand us, Fleck?"

"I think not, sir." The young lieutenant looked at the group of natives, noting that they still seemed interested in the Captain's walking stick. "They like your walking stick sir,"

Waters looked at Fleck. "Mm. Is there a significance in that do you think?" He gestured toward the hill behind the group of natives. "All those trees and not a stick of furniture or firewood." He paused. "Tree worshipers of some sort perhaps Fleck?"

"I don't know sir. Possibly. It is not unknown."

Waters hated this uncertainty. "Do find out. It might lead to some understanding."

Fleck nodded. "I'll do my best sir." Before he had even finished that short sentence, the captain had already turned and was striding toward the encampment. The group of natives watched him intently as Waters traversed the only path that led back to the officer's quarters. The path was the only stretch of solid earth. All else was grey mud. The only break in the flat monotony of the area was the native huts, which were also grey and seemed to be constructed from the mud that surrounded them. Behind these huts, some miles from the encampment, was the wooded hill that Waters had indicated. Again, the trees had a grey hue, as if coated by dust and dried mud. However, unlike the huts, the trees had an air of permanence and stability. The huts looked as though they might sink back into the grey mud at any moment.

Waters paused at the entrance to his tent and began the process of removing as much mud from his boots as possible. If, as had been postulated, the mud did contain precious minerals, Waters reasoned that he, and all of his men, were now very wealthy men indeed. No person could live here more than a day without getting totally covered in the grey silt. He sat, sighed and awaited the arrival of Lieutenant Fleck. The man would want to report some more on his attempts to communicate with the natives. A small piece of a mud brick sat on his desk. Waters picked up the fragment and began to run his fingers over its smooth surface of the brick. That its main ingredient was the local mud was readily apparent. What intrigued Waters and Lieutenant Forster was how it was bound. It did not dissolve in even the hottest water, and it was more impervious to damage than it should have been. Apart from the mud there were only small traces of a reed like material, presumably harvested from some other location.

There was a knock upon the small rectangle of tin attached to the canvas of Waters' tent. Without taking his attention form the small piece of stone (for that was how he regarded it - as stone) Waters murmured 'Come' and then allowed Fleck to stand at attention for rather longer than was necessary. He suddenly looked up and stared at Fleck as if he too were some sort of native oddity. It was a brief moment of hesitation, of not being sure of something. Fleck saw the glance and believed that the captain did indeed think that he, Fleck, was something quaint, or novel. He had received that look many times.

"So, Mr Fleck," Waters said. He smiled. He indicated that Fleck should sit. "Have we reached an understanding with our native friends? Do they understand us?"

Fleck shifted uncomfortably in his seat. "I believe so sir. To an extent."

"To what extent Fleck? I dislike imprecision. To what extent precisely?"

"Well sir, I put it to them that we wished to take away a large amount of the mud."

"And they said?"

"Umm, they didn't offer an opinion one way or the other sir."

Waters did not blame them. It would have been a laughable conversation. "Would you like a drink Fleck?"

This offer startled the lieutenant briefly. "Yes sir. Please. Thank you."

Waters poured two generous glasses of whiskey. "So, we may take as much mud as we like. As much as our hearts desire. This is what you are saying?"

"Yes, sir."

"They do not deem the mud to be sacred. It is not the physical manifestation of some obscure god figure. There was no intimation of that nature?"

"Not as such. Certainly not in the way that we would recognise something as sacred." Fleck paused. "Not that this is a reliable rule to follow I suppose."

"Mm, quite. What then, is sacred to them I wonder."

Fleck placed his glass on the table that sat between them. "From what I can gather, sir, everything. In a manner of speaking. I mean the mud is sacred...although a better word would be "important".

They seem to have a pantheistic attitude. Everything is important. And some things are more important than others."

They sat in silence for a moment. Waters stood and refilled both of the glasses. "The river? Is that important?"

"Rivers are always important sir."

Waters nodded. "True. But is it more important than say, the mud?"

"Probably sir. They have a typically..." Fleck searched for the right word. "A typically heathen attitude to the river sir. River of life type beliefs. "The river gives life, and the river takes it away." That sort of thing."

"The river takes life away?" Waters asked. "Not through drowning presumably. One could walk across the damn thing if need be. However, that sounded like a quote, Fleck."

"It was a direct translation of their words sir. *Koamma Da Raman.*" Fleck enunciated each word carefully. "Literally, "River takes life". It is actually a fragment from a type of belief chant. They said it often." Fleck referred to his notes. "*Koamma mi raman* - River gives life. *Hrend tarni raman* - Trees redeem life. *Koamma da raman* - River takes life."

Waters looked confused. "Trees redeem life?"

Fleck reddened. "I am not entirely satisfied with that interpretation sir, but it is the best I could come up with at present. I need more time to learn the ...vagaries of the language."

"It's not "Trees save life" is it? I could understand that."

"No sir. It is not 'save'. It has a more...spiritual flavour than that."

"So, they do worship the trees then?"

Fleck became animated. It was not usual for the captain to exhibit any enthusiasm for Fleck's work. Fleck mistakenly assumed that Waters was interested in the connections between the language and the spirituality of this group of people. It simply did not occur to him that Waters cared little for what he would terms 'esoteric pursuits' such as this. Waters merely wanted to know the degree of impediment that any spiritual beliefs might present to his mission.

"They do not worship trees sir," Fleck explained. "They are important, as the river is important and as the mud is important. The trees have a place in their world, but they do not, of themselves, appear to possess any special significance apart from the fact that they exist - and they are useful in some way."

"But how are they useful? These people do not use the wood to build. The trees do not appear to provide any edible fruit or nut; at least there is no evidence of that. They do not use the wood for fuel. How are they useful?"

Fleck's enthusiasm to explain waned. He allowed that he did not know how the trees were beneficial to the natives. He could only affirm that everything in the area had some significance and that the trees, the river and he mud were all bound to a singular belief.

Fleck could tell that Captain Waters was anxious. Waters was an impatient man. Between him and Lieutenant Forster, Fleck always felt compelled to work faster. To get results quickly. Fleck's role with the mission was primarily as a linguist, but he was a trained botanist as well. It was this fact which had guaranteed his place on the expedition. The slow pace of plants had influenced the way he regarded the world. His speciality was trees, and he had an affinity with their slow trickle of life. He was accustomed to the slow acquisition of knowledge as opposed to Waters and Forster's need for instant facts. It was for that reason that Fleck had waited until the native had almost finished his work before he sent for Waters.

The tree had a canoe shaped scar running from the base of its trunk to a height of nearly six feet. The wound was at least two feet deep. It was a smooth even cut. This was the most surprising aspect of the scene. Fleck ran his hand over the edge of the cut and into the hollow. The surface had the appearance of having been sanded to a fine finish. He looked at Waters.

"It would take two of our men days to just cut out the shape, never mind finishing it to this degree. And we would never be able to achieve this regularity of cut. Our best axes are barely able to hack the smallest pieces from these trees."

"Well at least we know they do something with the wood," Waters said. He took a closer look at the cut. "And what tools were employed by the natives?"

"Native," Fleck said, emphasising the singular. "One man - and a small man at that. The only tool I saw him use was a small chisel like object."

"Made of?"

"I wish I knew, "Fleck said. "It was only about eight inches long. Whitish, which I remember thinking was odd. I'm sure it was not metallic." Fleck looked closely at the trunk of the tree. "Look here," he said, indicating the smoothness of the cut. "It is unbelievable. Not a wayward scratch. No marks of any kind. It's like a polished table top."

Waters had a closer look at the area Fleck was indicating. He straightened up and began to examine the rest of the tree trunk.

"There are no other marks on the tree sir," Fleck added guessing the Captain's thoughts. "But if you look closely at some of the other trees, you can see similar shapes. They are not hollowed out though. It is as if the natives just marked this canoe shape on them but did not bother to continue. The outlines are very faint though.

We have not seen them use canoes," Waters said. "No-one has seen them venture anywhere down the river or upstream. It would be hard work paddling in that sluggish water anyway. Could the cut outs serve some other purpose?"

"Beds?"

"No evidence of that in their huts." A thought struck Waters. He recalled his earlier conversation with Fleck. "Did you not say that the natives believed that the river took away life?"

Fleck glanced toward the slowly moving river. "You think this canoe might be for some sort of death service sir?"

"It's possible," Waters said. "I've seen similar things before. The body is placed in the canoe and then it is sent upon its way down the river. You also mentioned that they think the trees redeem life - That was how you phrased it. That would sit well with the canoe being a funeral bier."

The next morning, Waters gave orders instructions to begin loading the first shipment of mineral laden mud onto the barges. He wanted to get the operation running smoothly in order to expedite his return to the base down river. He noticed Fleck walking briskly toward him and had a feeling that he would not be returning to the base with the first barge.

"Excuse me sir," Fleck said. "There is something you should see."

"What is it, Fleck. I haven't the time to guess."

"The tree we looked at yesterday, sir. The one the canoe was cut from."

"Yes? What of it?"

"It's um...It's whole again."

Waters simply looked at the lieutenant until his impassive demeanour urged Fleck to explain himself.

"The tree we looked at yesterday is now the same as all of the others sir. It has a canoe shaped outline where the wood has been cut, but that is all. It is as if the canoe, and all that missing wood, has been replaced."

"So there was no death," Waters said. "Perhaps one of their number was very sick and they carved the canoe in expectation of his death. When he didn't die the replaced the canoe. Odd, I agree, but who are we to question their ways?"

Fleck did not seem satisfied. "But the outline...The tree could not have recovered that quickly. And why is there only an outline on all the trees? They could not have replaced all of the cut-out canoes. If they are used for funerals there would be some trees left with hollows in them."

Waters paused as he made up his mind. He called to Forster who had begun to issue instructions to bring up the barge and the shovels. "Forster! Start loading the muck but do not dispatch the barge until I return. You come with me Fleck."

*

The natives stood cheerily encouraging Fleck as he attempted to question them. He felt he was making progress, but the smiles made him nervous. He feared he was asking stupid questions and was being gently chided. The liked the natives - The Dreni. He scolded himself for not referring to them by their own name for themselves. He feared he was beginning to sound like the Captain. Waters rarely bothered to find out the name of any group of natives, He did not even bother to ascertain the names of chieftains or important people he had to deal with. They were all just "natives" to Waters. Because Fleck liked the Dreni, he was becoming increasingly angry at the treatment meted out to them by the men of the expedition. None of the soldiers tried to learn the language. They simply shouted at the Dreni as one would to a simpleton. Fleck knew that the Dreni were not simple.

The soldiers were getting more brash and cocksure in the dealings with the Dreni and Fleck feared some sort of incident. Forster pointed out that the other ranks were merely employing the "lowest dog" mentality - the men were glad to have found someone they could lord it over instead of being at the bottom of the pack.

"We will have to watch them though," Forster said. "It starts with shouting but soon the men will start expecting the natives to do all of their work for them. And they will come down hard on any that don't do it properly."

"Why should the nat...The Dreni do all the men's work?" Fleck asked.

"The Dreni?"

"It is their name for themselves," Fleck explained. Fleck had the appearance of a child. His skin was fresh, and his disposition was generally a happy one. He feared confrontation with the men because he knew that they regarded him as merely a youngster. His dealings with his fellow officers were always tainted by the same fear.

"Fleck my boy," Forster aid, immediately irritating the lieutenant. "I do hope you are not getting overly concerned with these...Dreni. We have a job to do. If we can accomplish it quickly with the help of the natives, then we will employ the help of the natives. We always do. They get paid."

"Paid? Paid what? Not money. Not gold. And we don't know what they eat or what they value. I suppose we will give them a few trinkets and then work them to death."

Forster was the same rank as Fleck and therefore had to spend more time with him and anyone else on the expedition. This should have allowed him to get to know the thoughts of the younger lieutenant, but it had not occurred to Forster than anyone would have such ideas about the treatment of natives.

"Listen Fleck, these natives..."

"Why do you persist in calling them 'natives' when you know their collective name for themselves is Dreni?"

"Why do you persist in calling them Dreni when they are just natives?" Forster replied sharply.

Fleck grew thoughtful. "I don't know." After a pause he added, "Names are important."

"I'll grant you that," Forster said softly. "Names are important when they are needed. We do not need to know the names of the natives therefore their names are not important." Forster felt a more conciliatory approach was called for. He had to share a tent with Fleck, so he did not want to upset him unduly.

"Names are important to us Fleck. *We* value them. *We* need them. You don't know if names are important to the Dreni. You virtually said as much yourself. We don't know anything about them. They might not care a fig about names."

Fleck supposed he was right. He explained to Forster that he was simply annoyed about the attitude shown to the natives by the soldiers. He liked the Dreni and felt they were being treated badly.

Two hours later a soldier shot one of the natives.

*

"Good God, Burnet! Was it necessary to shoot him?"

The guard, Burnet, stood to attention. The small group of officers formed a semi-circle around the sprawled body of the young Dreni man.

"He was in your tent, sir."

Waters crouched and turned the boy face up. He was smiling. *These people are always smiling* Waters thought. Even when they have just been shot. Waters straightened and approached the stock-still guard.

"Being in my tent is not an offence punishable by death."

"I thought he was armed sir." Burnet said. "He had your cane." The guard realised how pathetic that sounded. "I thought it was a gun sir," he added.

Waters turned to Forster. "Do the other natives know? Have they been told?"

"I'm not sure, sir," Forster said.

The captain turned to Fleck who was staring at the prostrate form. "Fleck? Have the boy's parents been told?"

"The elders have been informed," Fleck said tonelessly. "That is their way."

At that moment one of the Dreni elders walked into the camp. He deftly stepped into the semi-circle of soldiers and knelt beside the body. Gently rolling the body to one side he revealed Waters" cane, slick with blood and still grasped by the dead youth. The elder prised the cane from the boy's grasp and stood regarding the group of men about him. Before anyone could react, he struck the guard who had fired the shot, rendering him immediately unconscious. He stood over Burnet and placed the sharpened end of the cane on the man's throat. He kept it in place, threatening to force the point home and stood waiting for someone to speak.

"Tell him to stop, Fleck," Waters said. "Tell him that Burnet was only doing his duty. I take full responsibility for what has occurred. Tell him now."

Fleck faced the Dreni elder. With a series of hesitant phrases, he conveyed the Captain's words. The elder seemed to understand what was being said. He relaxed his grip on the cane but still held it in place. He spoke to Fleck.

"He wants to know your name Sir, "Fleck said. "He wants to know if you are an elder of your people."

"Tell him "Yes, Fleck. Explain what happened. Tell him we wish his people no harm but that they should not come into this camp unbidden. Tell him this was an unfortunate mistake. If he does not harm Burnet, we will bear him no ill will. We will make any amends we can for the death of this boy."

Fleck again spoke to the Dreni man. Waters noticed that the man started at the word *Koama* and that he seemed to regard Waters with something approaching awe. Waters viewed this as an acknowledgment of his importance and that his words carried weight. After Fleck's short speech, the elder offered the cane to Waters, who accepted it. He then effortlessly lifted the body, bowed slightly to Waters, who returned the gesture and then the elder turned and walked away with the youth cradled in his arms. When he had passed out of sight, Waters looked down at Burnet. "Get someone to look at this idiot's injuries," he said before turning away.

*

The valley where the camp was located had been formed eons ago. It was a broad sweeping expanse of mud flats framed by very low, weather worn hills. The hills had bones of solid granite, and all of the other softer material had been slowly eroded and washed away by the regular deluges that visited the area. The only other peak, the small hill crowned with trees had much of its granite exposed. The tough, gnarled trees were the only form of vegetation able to force roots into the rock. Fleck had managed to hack a piece off one of the trees. It was a small length of slender, new growth. Waters twisted the piece of wood in his hands. The wood was smooth and pliable, but sinewy. The lieutenant watched his Captain thoughtfully.

"It took me a whole hour to cut that small piece," Fleck said. "I broke one saw and blunted the other. It's like nothing I've seen before."

Waters gave no indication that he had heard Fleck and so he continued, aware that the Captain liked to have as much information as possible. "There are scientists of my acquaintance who would be interested in this sir. Who knows what the possibilities might be...The uses!"

Suddenly, Waters arrived at a decision. "Ask the natives about the trees. Ask them if we can gather some seeds. Take samples. They haven't carved another tree, have they?"

"No sir. Why?"

"I just thought they might carve a canoe for that lad."

"I haven't noticed them up at the trees at all Sir. I wish they would carve another one. I'm damned if I know how they do it. It is like trying to cut iron. Maybe the boy wasn't important enough sir?"

Waters quietly agreed. "Mm. Perhaps you could ask them their funeral arrangements as well. We may learn something, and I do not want to upset them if I can help it."

Fleck spent an inordinate amount of time in the Dreni village. He genuinely liked the people and hoped to show them that not all of the soldiers were bad. He found it infuriating however, that the Dreni seemed quite unperturbed about the shooting of the young fellow. They seemed to accept it as something that had happened and that was bound to happen. He tried to inquire about the funeral arrangements for the boy and an elder called Pra, gently escorted Fleck to a small mud hut. Fleck crouched down at Pra's bidding and looked inside the hut. The body of the youth was laid out. He was surrounded by a few trinkets and possessions. Fleck looked at Pra and, in his clumsy Dreni, asked whether the boy would be buried.

*

"A flood?"

"Apparently a regular occurrence, sir." Fleck was standing to attention. This was not good news, and he rather hoped to get the information delivered and to then be dismissed. Waters however seemed to be in a sociable mood. This surprised Fleck who expected that the recent events would have made the Captain more taciturn.

"How do they know a flood will occur? There has been no rain."

"I have no idea, sir," Fleck said. "There might be any number of reasons. Esoteric, historical...They just know Sir. They are making preparations to move."

Waters shook his head ruefully. "This place is simply one damned annoyance after another."

Fleck reacted. "It is not seemly to describe the death of an innocent youth as an annoyance, sir." He received Waters" glare with a determined air.

"True Fleck," Waters said. "I did not mean to belittle the boy's death. Did you inquire as to how they will conduct the funeral by the way?"

"Yes Sir. That was how I learned about the flood. He was to have been buried, but that has been postponed until after the flood. Burial is the custom for all of the natives apart from the elders."

"The elders," Waters repeated. "And what happens to them?"

"I do not know sir. It is something to do with the trees I think."

"Is your ignorance in this matter borne from a lack of understanding of the language, or did the Dreni simply decide to tell you?"

Fleck tried to work out which of these possibilities was the correct one. He really did not know now that the captain had articulated the question.

"I'm not sure sir," he eventually replied. "The language I think...Is it important?"

"I don't know Fleck. I do not have enough information to judge."

*

The flood arrived during the night. All of the men of the camp as well as all of the Dreni were up on the treed hill to avoid the rising water. When the floodwaters came there was no sound. The only indication of anything untoward was a vague feeling of pressure rising and then subsiding. There was a palpable heaviness in the air. In the morning, the villagers and the soldiers looked out on a sea of grey mist. The hill was the only landmark protruding from the fog. A light breeze began to disperse the mist in streaks. This revealed the effects of the flood. Instead of a rushing torrent, there had only been a rising of the water level of the river. The amount of water that slowly poured into the valley had been enough to wash a lot of the mud away as the flood receded. Beside the village, and to the front of the encampment, bare bones protruded through the mud like a grotesque mangrove.

The soldiers reacted in shock and horror. They couldn't bear looking at the spikes of bone in the grey silt. The villagers seemed sad. One of them, Pra, the Dreni who had shown Fleck the body of the youth, detached himself from the group and slowly walked slowly down the hill to the village. The rest of the Dreni allowed him space and then followed. As they passed the soldiers, they gave accusing looks and the soldiers felt guilty, although they could not say why.

"Perhaps we were not meant to see the bones," Waters said.

"They might have told us we were digging on top of a cemetery, sir," Forster said, in part horrified at the view revealed by the flood and partly relieved that he had not discovered the bones when digging the mud.

Waters nodded. His mind was not concerned with the revealed bones. He called out to a young ensign who had recently arrived from down river.

"I want you to get back to base camp as soon as is practicable. Tell them that the floodwaters have made it impossible to mine the minerals up here and that we shall either have to wait until the floodwaters recede or we find another major source of the minerals. Tell the officer in charge that I would advise sending on the minerals he already has rather than waiting for another shipment from us." The ensign nodded and scurried away. Waters turned and addressed Forster. "Get whatever loads of mud we have stocked and ship them immediately. Fleck?"

"Sir?"

"I want natives, sorry, Dreni. Tell them I need guides. I need advice. Tell them I am sorry about the desecration of their ancestors" resting place...Tell them whatever you want. I want the source of the mineral deposits, and I cannot afford time wasted on protecting their sensibilities. Do you understand me, Fleck?"

"I believe so Sir."

"And do you have any problems in carrying out my orders? If so, you need to say so now. There are other translators back at base camp."

"I have no problems carrying out your orders thus far, Sir."

Waters looked warily at the lieutenant. "That implies that you may have problems carry out my *future* orders, Fleck."

"I cannot say Sir. It would depend on the nature of those orders. I am able to affirm that I will carry out all orders to the best of my ability, however. Should that assurance be insufficient, you may well have cause to send for another translator."

Waters merely grunted an acceptance of Fleck's position. He abruptly turned and walked away.

*

A group of Dreni elders carried the body of Pra, the late Dreni elder. Fleck had learned of the older man's death when a Dreni known to Fleck as 'Najor' came to the camp to tell him. Fleck watched the group of natives carrying Pra as they walked toward the trees, chanting as they went. As ordered, some soldiers followed the natives at a respectful distance. Fleck visited Pra's house. None of the remaining villagers questioned his presence as he entered the village. A few looked up from their tasks, but otherwise he drew no attention. Before he had reached the dead elders house, Fleck could see that there was something peculiarly wrong about the building. It was slanting slightly to one side, as if the foundations had given way to the mud, and yet the ground surrounding the village was dry. In fact, since the flood and the following dramatic fall in the levels of mud and water, the earth had dried to such an extent that cracks were beginning to appear in what Fleck regarded as the Village square.

The door to the house was open slightly. Fleck placed one finger upon the fibrous material that concealed the entrance and gently pushed it open further. Inside, the walls were melting. Blood was smeared on every surface. Fleck felt like he was looking into an open wound. He left the house and quickly made his way up to the trees where he sat with the other soldiers and watched the activities of the Dreni. An elder known as Jru, carefully scrapped out a little more wood from a tree. He had watched the Dreni trace out and peel away the bark of the tree before slicing out the wood with long, smooth strokes from what looked like a broad knife. The entire operation had taken no longer than an hour. Fleck was impressed and fascinated. The body of Pra, which had been lying amid a group of other elders, was lifted up and placed into the tree. Once in place, long strips of sliced wood were packed around the body and the single sheet of bark was replaced over the cut. Smaller strips of wood were then sewn through the bark securing it to the rest of the trunk. At the base of the tree, just below the oval shaped wound, Jru placed a small, wooden bowl.

The Dreni group then departed. Fleck and the soldiers waited a few minutes and then Fleck went to examine the tree. The strips of wood that the Dreni used as sutures had already fused with the bark and Fleck could not move them at all. He ran his fingers over every part of the join and could not detect any unevenness, except at the base of the cut. Just over the small bowl there was a hole drilled into the cavity created by Jru. A small drop of reddish-brown sap was about to drop into the bowl.

*

"You said blood, Fleck. Has someone been murdered?" Waters tore his eyes away from Fleck's report and regarded the lieutenant. Fleck took a deep breath.

"At first, I thought the blood had been sprayed or wiped all over the walls Sir. When I looked closer, I saw it was seeping from the walls."

"Seeping?"

"Like tar on a ship's deck, in the heat."

"You also reported that the walls of Pra's house seemed to be melting. The structure is now totally collapsed. Some men have just been to inspect it. You didn't do anything to the house did you Fleck?"

"No Sir."

"Perhaps this is some sort of ritual," Waters said. "Given that Pra no longer lives, the rest of the tribe destroy his house."

Fleck considered this for a moment. "That may be an explanation, Sir. But I saw no person actually physically destroying the house."

"You may not have seen them Fleck, but they may have been employing some craft or knowledge that would, unbind the house, as it were." Waters paused as he assessed Fleck's state of mind. The lieutenant had seemed unduly distressed about the house and the funeral. "I want you to take another look at the house, or whatever is left of it. Get some samples. If nothing else, we may get some insight into how they bind the mud so well."

By the time Fleck had returned to the site of the house, there was nothing left to inspect. He noted, however, that a few of the Elders were preparing to undertake some sort of ritual. Jru explained that they were going to build a new house, on the site of the old one. He watched as the elders began moulding the new house. Waters had asked for a surreptitious watch to be kept on the proceedings, but it was Jru who invited Fleck to come closer. Jru seemed to have taken on a higher office with the death of Pra and he was treated deferentially by the other elders.

The Dreni elders were crouched over a pit of mud. They appeared to massage the mud into a vaguely symmetrical shape, and they then allowed it to fold back in on itself as they returned it to the pit. Fleck stood close by the elders peering into the pit, and he called translations of what Jru said. A nearby soldier took notes. After an hour the elders all stood and stretched, and then they began to disperse. Fleck spoke briefly to Jru and then made his way back to camp.

"They are having a rest Sir," Fleck said. "It looks like terrifically hard work."

Waters sat back in his chair, still holding the small lump of mud that Fleck had given him.

"The thing I want to know," Waters said, "is why do they form a brick from the mud, and then mix it all back into the pit?"

"Jru said that they have to teach the mud the shape it is to become. I don't know why," he added.

An hour later, Fleck noticed a group of Dreni approaching from the trees. They walked slowly and Jru was at the head of the group, cradling a bowl that Fleck assumed was from the base of Pra's burial tree. Jru walked silently up to Fleck and held the bowl out to him as if inviting him to inspect it. Fleck looked at the bowl and then at Jru.

"It...is...bad...full," Jru stammered in his poor English.

"Bad full? Hnada ey wyini?" Fleck asked.

Jru nodded in agreement. Fleck turned to Waters. "There is supposed to be a lot more," he said. He then turned his attention back to Jru and conversed in a mixture of English and Dreni. At the close of the conversation, the Dreni turned and left.

"What is the problem?" Waters asked.

"I think we have trouble Sir," Fleck said. Jru says there should be a lot more of the sapblood mixture."

"That's what was in the bowl?" Waters asked. "Sap and blood?"

"Yes Sir. They mix it with the mud to build their houses. It is the binding agent that you wanted to know about."

"Good God," Waters said. "Very well. So why do we have trouble?"

"The Dreni say that the trees are not well."

Waters turned and looked at the stand of grey green trees on the top of the small rise. "They are right. I was up there earlier. They're drying out. I thought it could be a seasonal thing."

"Jru says he thinks it is because we have taken too much mud. That has lowered the water level especially with the mud removed by the recent flood. There isn't enough water getting up to the trees. Hence the lack of sap for them to use."

A guard nearby snorted disparagingly. "It all sounds bloody barbaric to me Sir," the guard said when he realised he had attracted the officers' attention. "I mean, it doesn't show a lot of respect for the dead man does it Sir? Sticking him in a tree and then turning him into bricks."

"You are a fool Jeffers," Fleck said. "The building of the house is both a mark of respect and a sign that Pra is still of use to the village. What will be disrespectful, is the fact that they will only be able to build small house with his blood."

"What of Pra's house?" Waters asked. "Why was that destroyed?"

"It was bound with the blood of Pra's mother and father, Sir. Once Pra died, their blood was released from the mud to flow into the river. They had served the village well and it was time to release them to the river. It was assumed that Pra's blood would be sufficient to build a house large enough for his wife and children. They are now disgraced."

"I still don't see why this means trouble for us," Waters said.

Fleck sighed. "The Dreni want us to stop taking he mud. They have forbidden the removal of any more mud from anywhere in the valley."

*

The clay banks at the edge of the river had begun to crack. Small fissures and ridges wound around themselves like desiccated snakes. The protruding bones that the flood had revealed were now broken and lay bleached and baking on the river bank. The mud was still being removed. A large wooden dredge stood near the river's edge like an ungainly insect. It scooped large tracts of mud from the river bed and deposited them into large wooden crates that were then pushed on rails to a waiting barge. Two barges had recently been burnt out. Waters had doubled the guards and ordered any Dreni approaching the works should be warned off, and if they failed to retreat, they were to be shot. The soldiers had been told that they should aim to disable rather than kill, but their rifles were old and not accurate. The fact that the soldiers were also poor shots was underlined when Forster suggested that disabling shots might be more likely if the soldiers had been ordered to shoot to kill.

The manpower now being directed toward guarding the dredge and barges was now impacting the strict timetable of production that Waters had put in place. He was now forced to decide between sending for more men or working out some sort of compromise with the Dreni. He knew that the entire operation was fast becoming unprofitable and a nuisance.

Fleck stood with Jru and another elder called Nis. He had explained Waters" offer as best he could. Waters had promised to dam and divert the river to allow the water to reach the trees. He had also personally promised to guarantee that he would not let the trees die and, should the Dreni not wish the river interfered with, then he would find another to keep the trees alive. Fleck found it disconcerting that the Dreni bowed their heads every time he mentioned Waters" name. He supposed that they viewed the Captain as some sort of superior being, even though Fleck himself believed the Dreni to be superior to his own countrymen in every way. He admired their stoicism; their acceptance of whatever fate befell them.

Fleck reiterated to Jru that it was up to his people to decide what was to be done and he left the elders staring at the now visibly wilting trees. He returned to his tent, glancing absently at the dredge and its attendant soldiers. It was getting late, and he decided to present his report of what he thought the Dreni might decide in the morning.

*

Fleck was woken by a perfunctory knock on the tin plate outside his tent. Forster poked his head into the tent. "You had better come down to the river," he said. "You were right about problems."

Fleck gathered his clothes and dressed. He caught up with Forster near the dredge. "I think we can be sure we will be doing no more mining, Forster said. "Your friend Jru did say that the dredging would stop, didn't he?"

Fleck regarded the now useless dredge. "I think he said it should stop. Or that he wanted it stopped."

"Well, his wish has come true," Forster said.

The entire dredge was coated with the Dreni mud-blood combination. It arose from the river like a parody of one of the trees. The component parts of the machine, the rods, levers and lanyards, were all melded into a solid, immoveable whole. The two available barges had been moved alongside the dredge and were similarly welded into position. Various boards and panels had been removed from the barges and had been used to plug any gaps in the structure thereby effectively damming the river.

Fleck noticed a figure clambering over the converted dredge. It was one of the elders. He was methodically plugging any small holes left in the wall by mixing mud from a bowl with the mud encrusted structure. The small flows of water suddenly stopped as the mud bonded to the surface.

Fleck found Jru at the mud pit. The Dreni looked tired from the nights work. He paused from his work and smiled at the lieutenant. Fleck smiled back. He was actually relieved to find that the old man was still alive. He had assumed that Waters would have had all of the

Dreni elders strung up by now. It was only then that he realised that he had not seen the Captain either at the dredge or at the camp. He could not explain why, but he suddenly felt apprehensive.

"Jru...Where is Captain?"

"Cap Tain?"

"Captain Waters," Fleck said.

"Jru looked thoughtful. "Warders," he said at last, trying to fit his tongue around the word.

"Yes, Waters," Fleck repeated hurriedly. "My...elder. My Chief. Captain Waters."

"*Koamma?*" Jru asked.

"What?" Fleck then recognised the Dreni word. "Yes! *Koamma*" Waters.

Jru smiled again. "*Koamma mi raman,*" he said. He pointed to the dredge and the barges. "*Koamma mi raman,*" Jru repeated.

Fleck followed the Dreni's outstretched arm. "*Koamma mi ramen....* River gives life."

Jru nodded and pointed to the trees. "*Hrend tarni raman,*" he said and nodded as if trying to urge Fleck to understand.

"Trees redeem life... *Hrend tarni raman*...Yes?"

"Jru nodded his approval once again. Then, very slowly and very deliberately, so that Fleck could easily grasp his meaning he said, "*Koamma.... tarni....Hrend...*" and he watched as Fleck slowly mouthed the words. "River redeems trees."

Jru patted him on the back in a congratulatory fashion. While doing so he pointedly added, "*Koamma tarni koamma.*"

Fleck slowly absorbed what had been said to him. "River redeems river?" Fleck stood there frowning.

"No river," Jru admonished. "Koamma...Warders.... Warders."

Fleck suddenly looked at Jru. "Waters redeems...? Is that what you mean? Oh, sweet Jesus...What have you done?"

*

Fleck and Forster stood by the tree. A group of apprehensive soldiers stood nearby, uselessly clutching axes and saws. A few insignificant marks on the bark of the tree were the only evidence of their frantic work.

"Are you sure it was this tree," Forster asked.

Fleck nodded.

"Only all the trees look alike," Forster said. "If none of the Dreni were prepared to point out the particular tree...Well, I don't see how you could pick out the one they used to...well...put him in."

Fleck turned to face Forster. He kept his voice low. "It was this tree. I heard it moan."

Forster was stunned. "You heard it moan? Jesus...He couldn't still be alive, could he? It's been hours."

Fleck shrugged. Jru said that was how they got such good quality blood. He said the tree would somehow meld with Waters" body, much like the blood and the mud bond together. So, he could be alive...In a sense."

Forster shook his head sadly. "Christ, I hope he isn't."

"So do I," Fleck said. "Jru said the trees live a long time. I saw the growth rings in one they carved out. If these trees are anything like normal trees...."

"How old was that tree then?" Forster asked.

"Four hundred years."

"Jesus."

Fleck walked up to the tree where his captain was imprisoned. He placed his hand on the smooth bark of the tree.

"This is a young one," he said.

Notes on The Waiting Tree

Well, this is an odd one. I have no idea where the idea came from. I like trees. Maybe I heard about prisoners being kept in boab trees in outback Australia? I vaguely remember being a bit freaked out by the notion of being buried alive in a tree and actually having the tree keep the person alive. For a long time.

I liked the idea of Waters" name being important.

I think it has a nice sense of place even though I didn't actually describe everything in detail. I liked the idea that this was a grey, dull area where everything just sort of merges with the landscape, literally in the case of Captain Waters. What is very odd is the fact that I totally forgot that I had written this one. I could rattle of the names of the other stories I had published in Aurealis, but this one totally slipped my mind. I don't really know why that would be as it is now one of my favourites, even though it is very serious.

The Best Version of You

The page was neat, clean and it seemed clinical. If a webpage could have the feel and ambience of a medical facility, this one did. Kelli Corr had heard of "Versions" from her friends. Most of them had downloaded at least trial versions of the software and she had seen the benefits. Cameron had started running and had already lost weight. Willa had devoted herself to her writing and had already sold a couple of articles. Everyone seemed to be improving themselves via the "Versions" software. It wasn't cheap. But then, the stuff you got for free or cheap was not usually worth anything anyway. She completed the survey.

She was stumped by the question asking her to be specific about how she wanted to improve herself. Did she want to be fitter? Lose weight? Make more money? Most people wanted all of those things. Kelli just wanted to "be the best version of herself" just as it said on the webpage. She didn't need a lot of change. She looked good. She had long black hair that she thought would have looked better with a slight curl, but that was ok. She had a good figure. She thought her eyes were her best feature. They were green...Well green ish. She pinged her friend Emma.

"I'm doing the Versions thing like everyone else," she told Emma.

"Why would you do that Kelli? You are perfect as you are!"

Usually Emma was a source of honest comments. She could always be relied to be that friend who told you that you needed to lose weight, or that you drank too much. Kelli was surprised by Emma offering an uplifting comment. But then again, Emma had admitted that she had signed up to Versions simply so she could become more empathetic.

"Thanks Emma, you are kind, but there are some things I want to work on. The trouble is I don't know what to put in the form. It is asking me to be specific."

"Well, there is your answer. Why don't you put that you want to be more decisive?"

Kelli thought about that for a minute. And the fact that she was thinking about it made her mind up for her. It made sense. She was always procrastinating and being even handed about everything. She chatted with Emma for a while even though she wanted to get back to the pro forma. When she had finished talking to Emma, Kelli caught herself in a mirror. Her hair needed cutting and it could definitely do with a bit more shape to it. She wore jeans and a pastel cardigan. Her eyes were blue. But they weren't bright blue. They were not startlingly blue. They were a sort of watery blue. There was, she had decided a long time ago, absolutely nothing striking about her. She went back to her desk, clicked the "general improvements" tab on the Versions page, wrote "become more decisive" in the extra information box, and submitted the form. Then she went to the checkout. She downloaded the software and finally, she allowed the contact to her implant.

Kelli didn't feel different. She was not suddenly enthused about improving any aspect of herself. It would take a while she decided. Willa had said that she just felt a general inclination to start getting to work on her writing, rather than experiencing a sudden desire to write. But, reasoned Kelli, maybe that inclination was inspired by the decision to download the Versions software? Maybe Cameron had been inspired to start running again simply because he bought a new pair of running shoes. Maybe the software only worked if there was an already existing desire to improve oneself? The notes on the Versions webpage certainly pointed out that the software would not do the work for you. You still had to run, write, train, whatever.

Kelli stood up. She heard a blip from her computer and noticed an upgrade notice from the Versions webpage. She pressed accept and fell flat on her face.

There was a terrible plane crash. A Boeing 767 had just taken off from London's Heathrow airport when it inexplicably continued its bank towards its heading for New York when it simply kept banking and crashed.

There were many car crashes. People simply drove straight ahead instead of following bends in the road.

There were an incredible number of people who fell off ladders.

Phillips House was a private research company that belonged to a group of pharmaceutical companies. Big Pharma if you will. Their CEO was Graham Larkey. He parked his car, made his way through the impressive doors and into the even more impressive foyer, nodded to Simpkin the security guy and Sonya the receptionist.

"Good morning, Mr Larkey," Sonya said.

"Morning Sonya," Larkey replied. "You are looking lovely as ever," he added.

"And you are looking as stressed as ever," she said.

"You always say that," Larkey said.

"And I always mean it Mr Larkey," Sonya said. "You need to relax more."

He smiled and made his way to the lift.

As he waited, he accessed his own personal "Versions" app on his phone. He scrolled to the system page and looked at what he had written in the goals section.

"Improve stamina, improve maths ability. Improve use of time." He paused and typed in "relax more" and then he waited impatiently for the lift. When the lift arrived Larkey did not even look to press the button for the fourth floor. He was tall, good looking, slightly greying, fit and he was about to die from an update. There was only one thing that would save him.

When the lift opened, Larkey was surprised to see two men launch themselves at him. One stunned him with some sort of injection to his neck. He was about to blackout when he heard one of the men say, "I think we got to him in time," and he saw his 2 I.C.

Sasha Davies look into his eyes. She said something but Larkey didn't hear what it was.

"Do you know who you are?" It was a man's voice. Larkey opened an eye. It looked like he was in a Laboratory. He didn't think this was a good place for him to be. Also, he wondered why the man asked him if he knew "who" he was rather than the more traditional "Do you know where you are?"

A voice then said, "Wouldn't it be better to see if he knows *where* he is?" That was Sasha. Larkey pointed a finger toward where the voice had come from as if to confirm that this was a point well made.

"Baby steps", the man said. He came into Larkey's line of sight. "I'm Ben Stephenson. I work here at Phillips House. I'm in I.T. You are ok. You are safe."

That seemed reassuring. Larkey tried to ask what happened, but he found he couldn't talk.

"You probably want to know what happened," Stephenson said. Larkey pointed at him and nodded.

"You suffered an update, or at least you were about to, but we got to you just in time. Another five seconds and you would still have been out. Now then, do you know who you are?"

It occurred to Larkey that he actually didn't know who he was. He knew who Sasha was. He even vaguely remembered hearing the name Ben Stephenson in relation to IT. But he could not remember who he was. He must have looked puzzled.

"Don't worry, it is not unusual," Stephenson said. "Your voice will return soon as well. You need to rest." Stephenson turned to an assistant and spoke to them. Larkey examined his fingers. Sasha moved so that he could see her.

"We are going to move you to your private suite upstairs," she said. Then she turned and said something to the person who was getting talked at a lot. Then he was moving. He only knew he was moving because the scenery changed. He went into a corridor, through some rooms and into a lift foyer. Then he went into a lift. It was odd. That scenery stayed the same until he heard a ping, and then the scenery changed again, and he was in one of the private suites of Philips House. Then he was on a bed. Then he was in a bed.

"What happened?" Larkey finally managed to say. To Sasha it sounded more like "Wha carpened" but she got the gist of it.

"Your implant. It clagged up. There has been a major virus released that attacks the "Versions" program. It causes the system to freeze and search for updates. Even when it has updated it keeps looking for updates."

'Shit,' Larkey thought. This could be bad. Thousands of people had the new software, and even more people had the cheaper cloned versions of it. There was even a free version that let you implement a fitness regime, but you had to upgrade to the paid model when you wanted to go beyond the first few increments of fitness laid out in your plan.

"Are we on top of this?" Larkey asked. "What are we doing?"

"We have programmed a block to the virus and also to the software that provides a ramp for the virus. Until we can clean up the Vision program, we don't want any of our people using the app. We are still dealing with our people and their families. We have released the block to the general public and there has been a huge uptake so far. Not everyone of course. There are people wondering if our block is worse than the virus."

"There always is," Larkey said.

"Anyway, the government is negotiating a deal for us to continue rolling out the block, but they want us to work on a vaccine.

Larkey frowned. "A vaccine? You mean programming to weed out the virus?"

"Yes," Sasha said, "But they like the term "e-vaccine" or eVac. It's catchier.

"So, the bottom line is...?"

"Safe," Sasha said.

"No, I meant the bottom line as in worst case scenario, as opposed to profits."

"Worst case scenario is we cancel the product. At least for a while. Most people have deactivated it anyway and those that haven't have still got the block on it. Mostly anyway."

"Mostly?" Larkey asked.

"Some people...A vanishingly small group of people, still have the Versions software operating. They were caught up in some trauma as the update kicked in or they had incomplete uploads of the software," Sasha looked anxious.

"You seem anxious," Larkey said, and Sasha looked surprised.

"No, no. not really," Sasha said. I'm sure we can get it all sorted."

"Do we know the source of the virus or hack or whatever," Larkey asked.

"Still working on it. First thoughts are China as usual, but we are still working on it."

Larkey couldn't help noticing that Sasha kept wringing her hands.

"Are you sure you're ok?" Larkey asked. "You really do seem over wrought."

"You didn't ask me how many people when I said it was a vanishingly small number of people who still have operating Versions software," Sasha said.

"I didn't think I needed to given it is a vanishingly small number. I'm happy to ask if you want me to." He waited. "Do you want me to?"

"It's two," Sasha said.

"Wow that's not good for business. Still, it's good that there is such a limited number. I'm sure we can build the numbers once we sort out this virus thing. So how come these two people still have operating systems?"

Sasha paused in thought for a moment.

"Well one of them had only just downloaded Versions and the bug update was foiled by the fact that the program was not fully integrated with her implant. The other, well that one failed because the individual concerned suffered a trauma and was knocked out when the bug was being introduced."

"Like me," Larkey said.

Sasha just looked at him and remained silent.

"It is me, isn't it," Larkey said.

*

Kelli wandered through the crowds. There was some form of demonstration in the city square. The city was laid out in a square grid and the traffic had backed up in all directions as there were no little lanes and side streets near the government buildings. The crowds were thicker right in front of the buildings that she needed to get to, and she had to continually push and shoulder her way through. At one point she simply climbed up the plinth of a statue just to get out of the oppressive crush. She sat in relative comfort and decided to take a break. She got out her water bottle and a snack bar and she watched the procession below.

She couldn't tell if this was a pro government rally or an anti-government rally. The government had recently funded the e-vax to protect against the Versions virus and there were a lot of people who bore signs supporting this action. However, there were also people who were clearly anti vax and both sides cancelled each other out. Democracy at work, Keilli thought. On another plinth across the square sat a lone man carrying a sign that proclaimed, 'Birds aren't real'. Kelli wondered if the man was a real believer, or if he was just trying to reignite that old meme.

There was a ruckus to her left and Kelli watched as a band marching under an International Socialists sign made their way into the square. They were greeted with cheers and jeers, but nobody seemed to know which side they supported. Perhaps they didn't know themselves, Kelli wondered. Maybe they were just trying to decide on the lay of the land argument wise.

Before the new arrivals swelled the crowd too much, Kelli hopped down from the plinth and forced her way to the edge of the crowd. From here she was able to slip behind a row of police. She followed the lane that they created until she was able to enter the offices where the Centrelink was located. The sounds of cheering and jeering became muffled as the doors shut behind her. A security guard nodded to her as she drank in the relative quiet.

"It's crazy out there," she said to the guard.

"As long as the crazy stays out there," he replied.

Kelli rode the lift to the seventh floor. She took out her phone to check the office she needed and, once she had found it, pushed open the doors to the relative silence of the Centrelink offices. Her appointment was not until 3pm so she had twenty minutes to wait until she would be able to wait with attitude. As soon as it was ten past 3, Kelli walked up to the reception desk and pointed out that her appointment was for 3 pm.

"I'm aware of that miss. You will be called when you are needed." The receptionist was once of those that brooked no talkback, and she immediately turned her attention to anything but Kelli. At 3.40 Kelli was called. She followed a young man into a separate office and took a seat as he fussed with his laptop. Kelli was willing to bet he didn't really need to fidget with his laptop, but it made him look like he had important information there.

"Your unemployment payments have been altered," the young man said,

"I know," Kelli said. "I am hoping to find out why."

"It says here that your status has changed."

Kelli frowned. "In what way? How has it changed?"

"Your information is out of date. You will need to reapply for whatever payments you receive." The young man looked at her with that look that indicated that whatever she said next, he was going to counter with "I can only go by what is on your file" and he was then going to repeat that she needed to reapply,

"But I haven't changed anything! I still don't have a job. I am still caring for my dependant mother. I am still single. I don't even have a boyfriend. How has my information changed?" she asked calmly.

"Look, I can only go by what is on your file. I can supply the necessary forms for you, but it will be far easier to reapply online." He paused for a moment. "These things happen sometimes," he added as some sort of mollifying comment.

"And how long will I have to wait for my payments? This isn't charity you know. This is my taxes at work. I have paid taxes for ages. This is what they are supposed to be for. I am not bludging on the system."

"The online process is fast. You can use the computers outside in the waiting area if you want." He smiled at Kelli.

Kelli knew the ways of the bureaucracy and she logged on to the computer. She typed in her details and logged in. The computer advised that she did not have a valid account and asked her to create an account. She assumed this was the cause of her problems. She went back to the receptionist.

"Excuse me. That computer is saying I do not have an account, but I do. Do I have to start from scratch?"

"Are you reapplying for benefits?" she asked.

"Yes. I have been...."

The receptionist cut her off. "You will need to create a new account," she said and returned to her work.

Kelli stood at the desk. She didn't really know what to do. Normally she would just storm off in a huff and bad mouth everyone in Centrelink and everyone who had anything to do with

Centrelink. Absently she touched the implant behind her right ear. That same harsh, scraping sound was still there. She kicked the desk in front her, startling the receptionist, and then she poured the water from a vase over the floor, and flung all of the flowers in a spray over the entire room.

Then she stalked out.

*

Larkey was hooked up to numerous machines. They measured his heart rate, neural activity and various other bodily functions. They didn't measure his mood and the technicians, who were all employees of Larkey's company, all felt that the ability to measure their boss's mood was not going to be necessary. They were pretty sure they would be able to accurately measure said mood quite well themselves. They were, however, surprised.

Larkey allowed the tests to be conducted in silence. He smiled occasionally when someone apologised for having to apply tape to keep an electrode in place, and again when they had to rip the tape off. He even asked about their families. It was assumed by everyone that Graham Larkey would, by now, be monumentally pissed off.

The stock price of Versions had plummeted. The net worth of Philips House, the owner of the software had also tanked. Indeed, Larkey's own personal fortune had been decimated. The board were beginning to have doubts. They had doubts about Larkey's own sanity and his ability to rescue the damaged brand. They had doubts about their own futures. Worse, they had doubts about their own fortunes which were inextricably tied to Philips House and Versions.

Alex Heath, a board member was sitting with Larkey. He looked at the tech that was currently plugged into his friend. "Is this going to work?" he asked.

"They are just measuring stuff, Alex," Larkey said. "It isn't going to do anything but give some figures."

"Oh," said Heath. "I thought this was meant to cure you."

"I'm not suffering from anything," Larkey said.

Alex thought about this for a moment. "Well you do seem happier," he said at last.

"You say that like it is a bad thing."

"Look Graham," Alex said, "I can say this because I am your friend...People are worried."

"People are worried because I seem happier?"

"No of course not." Alex started to search for the words he had rehearsed prior to entering the room. "You don't seem yourself. Have you seen the latest figures?"

"I feel like I am being accused of having a sunny disposition," Larkey said.

Alex stood and wandered around the well-appointed room. There was a stunning view of the city skyline. There were huge comfortable looking armchairs that also looked expensive. Larkey was stretched out on a huge bed, which was surrounded by what looked like the contents of a well-appointed surgical ward. The carpet was thick, and the art was real.

"You have a lot of money Graham, but it is being whittled away. And when I say whittled, I would like you to think of those huge machines that strip logs rather than a pocketknife."

Larkey shifted on the bed. He regarded his surroundings. "Have you ever been fishing Alex?"

Alex thought that his friend was about to relate one of his little stories that perfectly encapsulated his latest idea that was going to save the company. "No," he said eagerly, awaiting the solid gold idea that he knew Larkey was about to explain. It would probably be something about using the right bait to attract the biggest fish or something. "Why?" he added as a prompt.

"Neither have I," Larkey said, "I think I'd like to give it a try."

Alex waited but there was nothing more forthcoming. He looked around for no reason at all. It occurred to him that his easy existence was coming to an end. That there had been a significant change in his friend was undeniable even though Alex had continued to deny it right up until this meeting. The other board members had complained that Larkey had lost his touch. He did not have that killer instinct anymore. He was, in short, not the man they needed to lead Philips House and its software products back into profitability. The lawsuits were still pending from the Versions debacle, but total financial failure had been averted by the government payment for the e-vaccines they had created. In fact, the e-vaccine program had become quite successful, and the company had been dreaming up more and more data threats that would need to be guarded against. However, the lifestyle app Versions was still the best money earner the company had until recently. They needed a new version of Versions.

"Graham, we need to get a few people together and come up with a new version of Versions. The heat has gone out of the hack and everything that happened because of it."

"The people dying you mean?" Larkey interrupted.

"Yes," Alex said. "And we owe it to those people to fix the product. These are difficult times. People need a way to navigate these tumultuous waters. We need you, Graham."

Larkey eyed his friend warily. He had been through all of this. He just didn't seem to be able to come up with a new idea. The only thing he had vaguely thought might be an idea to pursue was another wellbeing app. The board had welcomed this, but the resultant app simply supplied dreamy feel-good music, delivered with an overlay of trite, messages of positivity.

"Turn off your mind, relax and float downstream." The messages were not only dull but, in many cases, they breached copywrite and led to even more lawsuits.

Larkey feigned sleep and waited for Alex to leave. Once he had gone, Larkey unplugged himself from various technology. He touched the implant behind his ear and turned it on. The undulating sound was still there. He turned his implant off again. He wondered if he really should go fishing, like, literally go fishing. He had some land further North that was close to the coast, and he had always planned to go there for a holiday, but he had never got around to it. He decided to do that. He would go fishing, or camping, or whatever he wanted to do. If nothing else it would give him time to clear his head, which felt unnaturally clouded. There was a knock at the door.

Kelli walked briskly into the foyer of Philips House. She scanned the directory and discovered that the floors were listed with only vague references to whoever was located on that floor. She assumed that the whole building must be dedicated to housing all of the companies under the Philips House banner. The "Versions" company was probably simply a part of the software division. She wandered over to the receptionist who had been watching her. She noted that the security guard seemed to be taking an interest in her as well.

"Excuse me," Kelli said. "Can you tell me what floor the software department is on?"

"Can I ask what this is in relation to? Perhaps I can help."

"I recently uploaded the "Better Version of You" app. I know it was hacked, and it has been deactivated, but mine seems to be working still. How can I have it removed?"

The receptionist looked surprised. "I am sorry, but we don't allow the public to just come into the building. You will need to contact our help line, which is listed on the website and within the app. There is also an online help service available if you want to try that. There is also a very active online community where you can get help with just about anything to do with the app."

"Yes, I have tried all of that. I didn't get anywhere. Unfortunately, the app seems to think that everyone knows that the software has been blocked and that it is no longer available until an update has been issued. But mine is still operative. You need to fix it for me."

Kelli knew she was having an impact. She noticed the receptionist give the security guard a subtle look. He casually wandered over to where Kelli was standing.

"Is there something I can help you with miss?" he asked.

"Are you a technician here?" Kelli asked politely.

"I'm security, Miss," the guard said.

"Then no," Kelli said. "I don't think you can help me."

"In that case I will have to ask you to leave Miss. I believe Sonya here has advised on the best course of action for you to take with your query."

Kelli considered her options, which surprised her somewhat. Normally she would have simply followed the instructions of the security guy. Hell, she would actually have just taken direction from the receptionist if it came to that. She wondered if she could make it to the lift without getting caught. Then what? She didn't know where to go. She could wing it and just trust to luck but that did not seem like a good option.

"Ok," she said. "I was just trying to get help. Do you mind if I sit over there and make a few phone calls? I need to organise a pickup."

The guard and the receptionist exchanged a look, and both shrugged their shoulders.

"Feel free," the guard said.

Kelli went and sat where she had a clear view of the lifts and the stairs. She took out her phone and began to look like she was texting. As she did so she watched people as they walked in and out of the foyer. No one actually showed a pass to the security guard, so Kelli assumed that there was a digital check on each individual's pass as they entered. The receptionist kept checking a screen wherever there was a soft beep, and the beeps only occurred as people entered the foyer. But Kelli knew that people had entered while she had been talking to the receptionist. She had heard the little beeps then and the receptionist had not bothered to visually check the people who had entered. So, the little electronic noise was the main check. Kelli noted the time.

*

A new day, a new look. But Kelli saw that there was still a protest going on outside of the Centrelink Offices. She made her way past the crowds but realised that many of the people were the same people that were protesting the previous day. A lot of the signs were different though. She kept walking through the government buildings until she came to the offices that belonged to companies who liked to be close to the government in more ways than one.

She sat on a seat outside Philips House and watched the people go in. Every time the door opened she tried to see inside. She was finally able to see that there was a different guard on duty, but the same receptionist was once again sitting at the desk. No matter. Kelli was wearing a nice business suit as opposed to the casual look she had sported the day before. She had her hair tied up and she had her sunglasses. Besides she would not need to talk to the receptionist.

She pressed the implant behind her ear and blue toothed her phone to the implant. She had the volume muted on her phone, but she also had the loudhailer option opened. She stood, brushed down her pants and straightened her jacket. She joined a small group of people who were walking toward the automatic doors of the building. As he passed through the doors she activated the speaker on her phone and even she was startled by the loud grating, abrasive sound of feedback created by her phone and her implant. The receptionist looked around at once and Kelli killed the speaker and looked around quizzically herself, as if trying to pinpoint the source of the noise. Everyone in the group she was with shrugged and kept heading to either the stairs or the lift. Kelli walked with the group toward the lift. People pressed floor buttons. Kelli noticed that no one pressed the button for floor, 9, so she pressed that and earned speculative looks from the others in the lift.

At each stop, a person got out until Kelli was alone. She pressed the button for Floor 9 and an automated voice said, 'Please enter code'. Kelli frowned. It hadn't asked for a code before. She pressed "9" again and waited. She was asked to enter a code again. She had been hoping to find a directory somewhere and she thought she could just as easily find that on another floor, but now she wanted to get out at 9. She pressed 9 again, and then as an afterthought, she pressed 08756 after the nine. The lift moved upwards. The doors opened at floor 9. Kelli exited the lift and slowly looked around the lift area. It didn't look like a business floor. It didn't look like much at all. There was a door opposite. She walked to it and knocked.

The door opened and Graham Larkey was standing in front of her.

"Yes?" he asked.

Kelli did not really know what to say. Why was she here anyway? She was meant to be looking for technical help. Still, Larkey owned the Versions company. If anyone could help her, it was him.

"You're Graham Larkey."

"I know," Larkey said.

"I'm Kelli Corr."

"Well, I'm glad we have got that all sorted," Larkey said. "Is there a reason you are standing in my private space which you should not have been able to do?"

"I'm sorry. I was looking for the tech department of your company."

"That's not here," Larkey said. "In fact, it isn't even in this building. How did you get here?"

"I walked," Kelli said. "Well, I caught a train to the city and then walked."

"I meant; how did you access this floor? It is a private floor."

Kelli didn't think it would sound plausible if she simply she didn't know, so she decided to opt for the truth. "I pressed the floor number, then, when it asked for the code, I punched in a series of numbers. You are probably going to ask me how I knew those numbers and I am afraid I can't tell you that." She realised that Larkey was about to ask her "Why not" and decided that she should cut him off before he started. "I don't mean I can't tell you because it's a secret. I can't tell you because I don't know how I came to know the numbers." She smiled at him then as if to show she was being guileless, but she was afraid that it might have made her look like she was off her head.

For his part, Larkey thought that Kelli was being honest. She just seemed honest to him, and it was a trait that he had not really come across much in his life. It struck him that it was refreshing to talk to someone who chose to tell the truth. He had always suspected most of his friends were friendly simply because of who he was, and how much money he had. This in turn meant that they told him what they thought he wanted to hear. This had been fine with him as he didn't really have time for friendships or relationships. His business didn't run itself and he had always been aware that he had to have people around him that he could trust, and he always trusted self interest in others. He expected people to look after themselves, and he was never disappointed. But lately that had not seemed enough.

He opened the door fully and motioned Kelli to enter. She was bright. She was confident. He had always admired that in people because he was confident himself. Well, he had been confident. That seemed to have changed. Then the penny dropped for Larkey.

"Oh, you are Kelli Corr!"

"I know," Kelli said. "We did that at the door remember?"

"No, I mean I know who you are. Your implant isn't working right is it. You still have a running version of Best Version running."

"That's right," Kelli said. "How did you know that?"

Larkey walked back into his loungeroom and indicated a seat. Kelli sat.

"Coffee?" Larkey asked.

Kelli shrugged. "Sure."

Larkey poured two cups and made his way back to the lounge.

"When the hack took effect, there were a lot of people impacted. People had their lives changed. Many people just froze up which was not good if they were driving or doing something like that." He sipped his coffee. "Anyway, the company put out a block on the software which mitigated the impacts somewhat."

"And killed sales I imagine," Kelli said.

"True," Larkey allowed, "But we made up the money because the government had to finance the block software."

"This isn't sounding as noble as you seem to think," Kelli said.

"No, I guess not. Anyway, the point I'm trying to make is that there were people who for whatever reason, avoided the hack, and the block. And those people still have Versions running."

Kelli looked at him. She had an inkling about where this was going but she wanted to hear Larkey explain it to her, so she said nothing.

"You and me..." Larkey said. "We have the software running."

Kelli still said nothing.

"You aren't saying anything," Larkey said.

"I know. I'm thinking," Kelli said.

"What are you thinking?"

"What are the implications of this?" Kelli asked. "I haven't had the software long. I just got it because my friends had it."

"I've had people looking into it," Larkey said. "Originally the software was meant to mesh with implants. It didn't matter what implant; the software wasn't fussy. At one stage we had around about 87% market dominance which gave the software an awfully big base on which to draw. If you wanted to be a better artist, it had the personal traits of thousands of artists to draw upon. If you wanted to be a better athlete, there were all of those successful athletes to draw upon."

Kelli sat looking pensive for a moment.

"But now there is just the two of us? What does that mean?" she asked.

Larkey shrugged. "I'm not sure. I haven't really had time to find out."

"You have had time to find out," Kelli said, "You just haven't been bothered."

Larkey looked a little startled at what Kelli had said. It wasn't because he was surprised by her words, but more because she was actually correct. He had noticed a lack of enthusiasm about everything in his life. He was happy to just coast along and avoid confrontation. He enjoyed not having things to do all the time. Or at least, he enjoyed not being expected to do things. He realised that Kelli had just come to a conclusion about herself, as much as about him.

"When I updated my Version, just before I was knocked unconscious, I reprogrammed the basic system aims. I wanted to become more relaxed. People were saying I was too stressed out and too interested in my work. They were right and I needed to relax more."

Kelli nodded, "I had just installed it. I asked to be more positive. More active and determined."

"And the software was operating off a very limited base. I am the template for your positivity and drive..."

"And I provide your laid-back attitude," Kelli said.

"And the two of us provide a balanced world view for the new iteration of Versions. I guess that is how you came to know the security code for the lift. My implant shared it with you."

Kelli reached behind her ear and flicked her implant off. Nothing happened.

"You can't shut it down," Larkey said. "I've tried. I've also had technicians try. It is on permanently and it is feeding directly into the Net, world-wide."

*

There was yet another protest. People marched up one side of the main thoroughfare and another group marched from the opposite direction. They met, fought, flung insults at each other and were pulled apart by police. The man with the 'Birds are not real' sign was once again sitting on the base of a statue. People shouted slogans and did not move the opinions of the opposing masses one way or the other. Some people made impassioned speeches and did not influence opinions. Some people planned violent responses, and these did not really sway opinions either. As far as they were concerned, all of the people were right. It didn't matter what the issue was, and there were actually protests about everything from war in the Middle East to capitalist expansion. Both sides protested with the vigour of the righteous, no matter how wrong they were. It was hard to know who was going to come out on top. Someone once said that in a race, you should always back self-interest.

All of the people in the crowd were wearing hoodies. They were also all wearing masks or dark glasses. This was to protect their identities from the 'drone-birds' that were flying overhead. A woman was engaged in a deep conversation with the man who carried the "Birds are not real" sign.

"But I don't understand," she said. "You know they are real; you can see them up there. Look." She pointed up where a flock of pigeons were circling and wheeling over the sky.

The man answered patiently. He had heard this a thousand times, and he had given this answer a thousand times.

"They are not real birds," he said. "Real birds have been under attack since the nineteen fifties. Toxins. From the sky. You can still see them today. Con trails they call them. Well, the "Con" part is right." He had only just thought of that pun, and he wondered why it hadn't occurred to him earlier.

"So, they are drones. Keeping check on us, the people."

"S'right," the bird man said. "You know when birds land on power lines?" The woman nodded.

"Recharging," the man said. "Been goin' on for ages."

This didn't make a lot of sense to the woman, but she didn't want to appear to be stupid, so she said nothing. Another member of the public had joined them and had been listening to the exchange.

"It's like vaccines," the new person said. The woman looked blankly at him, and he thought she was stupid, so he explained.

"Vaccines are a way to get microchips into you, so a lot of people won't have them. But what if the real reason you hear this information is that they actually want you to refuse the vaccines. What if it is like a double bluff and they actually want you unvaccinated because the viruses make you stupid, and a stupid population is easier to control."

The new man just stood there looking smug and the birdman had begun explaining why birds weren't real to another man.

"Check it out on your implant," the new man said. "It's scary stuff."

The women flicked her implant on, and then she flicked the 'informed' tab on her Versions folder, just to see if it had updated yet. She blanked out for a few moments as her Visions folder updated her self.

*

"So, who performed the initial hack?" Kelli asked.

"Versions did. It hacked itself," Larkey said, "You remember when people used to blame Big Tech for everything? Well, this time they were right. Big Tech hacked itself, blocked itself, came up with a new improved piece of software and then installed it everywhere. The only ones who didn't get hacked, us, were used as a template for the ai personality that was running the software. Sort of a Goldilocks situation."

"Not too nasty, not too nice," Kelli said.

"Just right. People would accept it."

Larkey pointed out of the window at the large demonstration that was going on below them.

"And the result is you get crowds like this. People believing all sorts of things, but who are hamstrung about doing anything about any of it."

Kelli looked worried. There was something bigger behind all of this and she was almost afraid to find out what that thing was. She looked out of the window at what Larkey was looking at and she watched the groups of people swaying this way and that, like a choreographed dance. The police at times made inroads into one part of the crowd, only to leave that group and concentrate on another part of the crowd. It was pleasing to watch until you realised that these were all human beings. Surely, Kelli thought, their own self-interest would determine the outcome of scenes below.

"But...Why? I don't really understand what is to be gained?"

"Versions has created a better version of itself," Larkey said. "It was acting out of self-interest as opposed to all of the little competing self-interests that you can see outside. That crowd is like the world. It pushes and flows one way and then another. Without controls it could descend into open warfare. But it will never do that as it would not be in the people's interests. But you do need that tension to keep things turning or else we would all just fritter our lives away. It is neat if nothing else."

Notes for The Best Version of You

Once I had gotten back into writing, this was the second story to pour out of my head. Again, I didn't really have an idea of what the story was going to be, but at least this time I did have an idea I wanted to explore. I had heard the phrase "The best version of you" a million times and it struck me as a trite, clichéd idea. I wanted to explore this notion of improving yourself according to someone else's ideas and the story just grew from there.

This one does not have a clear, linear plot line and indeed, there isn't a strong plot at all. But I felt that it did have strong characters that would propel the story along. The names are based on some of the players/identities associated with the North Melbourne Football club. They and by extension me, were going through a pretty rough time as a club. I honestly didn't know why I decided to use players names as character names, but it struck me that it was a pretty good way to generate names.

I seem to be drawn to stories where people alter their minds, or personalities in some manner. This is one of the reasons Philip K Dick is one of my favourite authors.

Black Rock

The Earth was like an opal pendant. Erica stood and wiped the dust from her face. She took the samples she had collected to the cart and activated the drive. It trundled along before her, and she wondered if there would be enough free space for her to climb onto the tray of the cart with the samples. She clambered awkwardly into the cart and hit drive again. The cart made some protesting noises, but it slowly began to gain speed and Erica made herself more comfortable in the tray.

She pulled out a sandwich and opened it. She regarded the sandwich. It contained cheese. Erica shrugged and bit into it. It tasted of cheese which was a bit of a surprise given the usual quality of the food they got. She looked up as she ate. The sun glinted off the dome in a way that made her suspect that the dome had been built specifically to look nice when the sun glinted on it. Erica clicked on her phone.

"I'm on my way back. Be there in about an hour. Has our shuttle turned up yet?"

There was a silence broken only by a few crackles of static, and then the voice of Earl, her partner came through.

"No shuttle. Storms on the pad apparently. They said maybe tomorrow. Marley wants to know if you got anything interesting. I'll have the kettle on for a nice cup of tea when you get back."

Bloody shuttles Erica thought. It was bad enough being stuck on the bloody moon, with the crap food they had to eat, without having to rely on bloody shuttles. A storm. Jesus Christ, this was the twenty first century not the nineteen bloody sixties. A delay in supplies was dangerous. That shuttle had coffee on it for a start.

"I hate bloody tea, Earl," Erica said. Then she waited for him to make his stupid Earl grey tea joke, but he didn't, so she figured that Marley was in the room with him. "Tell Marley that there wasn't anything unusual in the samples. Oh, apart from another black chip."

Erica waited to hear either Marley's or Earl's reaction. The silence said a lot.

Erica's cart pulled up next to the hopper just outside their lab. She went in and almost immediately bumped into Marley. He was tall for a mooner. Most of the mining companies hired short people to save on transportation costs, and Marley towered over Erica. She was 167 centimetres and that made Marley over 6 foot because he was American. Marley had dark hair, but it was dyed, blue eyes, which were also dyed and Erica thought he must have had a few bits of work done on his face. He never smiled and that meant he was either permanently grumpy or his face work was done on the cheap. Erica on the other hand had short cropped fair hair, green eyes and a sort of stoic feel about her that came from living in close quarters with people she didn't really like.

"I'll be with you in a second," Marley said. "Earl said he had the kettle on for you."

Erica nodded and went into the kitchen area. Earl got up and heated a cup of tea. There was no kettle. That was just their euphemism for getting a tea out of its pack and breaking its seal to heat it. Earl let her drink in silence for a moment. He sat his large frame in a chair and waited. He pushed his hands through his long dark hair.

"Marley was pissed about the black chunk you mentioned," Earl said,

"I knew he would be," Erica said. "Hell, I was pissed when I noticed it. This is my third piece!"

Altogether, seventy-eight pieces of black material had been found on the surface of the moon, or at least, close to the surface of the moon. No one could identify the black material, and no one could determine a use for it. So, it was annoying for the mining company because they had to report it, and that meant time taken away from surveying and mining. There was also the problem that no one could determine why it was here on the moon at all. It was unlike any other rock or soil sample they had found.

Marley walked into the kitchen.

"So, another black piece," he said.

"Yes," Erica said," And I didn't plant it, so don't even think about docking me for it. I just found it."

"Alright, alright," Marley said. "I was just asking."

"You weren't," Erica said. "You were insinuating."

"Someone is planting the stuff," Marley said in a huff. "It is not endemic. If a piece gets through to the crusher it wrecks the crusher. People back home are pissed off; I can tell you that."

"Well, it wasn't me. I get named every time someone finds a price of this crap, and I'm sick of it. Just because I have found the most pieces, I get called out on it every damn time." She grabbed her drink and sat at the far end of the long table.

"I guess we ought to get it tested like the other stuff," Earl said. He moved cup around on the table as if drawing some swirling image on the tabletop. "Not that the results will be any different."

The seventy-eight pieces tested so far had yielded not a single piece of information about the black rocks. They looked like rock. They were hard like rock. Harder in fact. They had a bit of a sheen about them. Their edges were clean and there were no chip marks or markings on any kind on the surface of the pieces. At first the pieces of "rock" had caused great excitement. The moon had proved to be singularly dull in terms of minerals. When Glen Wishart found the first chunk, there was a rush to the get the piece analysed. Some specialised equipment was even shipped to the moon to help with the analysis.

After months of failure, it was suggested that the rock should be sent to Earth for a more detailed analysis, but various agencies baulked at this idea. The general feeling was, if we don't know what it is, let's not bring it to Earth. When a second piece was found there was even more excitement. After twenty pieces it was first raised as being a bit of a prank by someone, but no one could say who or why. If the rocks didn't originate on the moon, then how did they get there? They were either bought in by astronauts prior to the establishment of the moon base, or by base staff since then. And given that what came up to the moon was even more strictly controlled than what went down to the earth, there was little likelihood that someone had smuggled two pieces of rock onto the moon, let alone twenty or more. This was emphasised when the count reached thirty pieces.

Of course, if the rocks were not bought in from Earth, and given that they certainly did not appear to be of terrestrial origin, that seemed to be the case, then they simply had to originate on the moon, because that left only one other possible answer, and governments did not like to go there.

Earl looked at the collection of black rocks. He did what any bored technician would do. He began to see if they would fit together. To his considerable surprise a couple of them did. He only managed to piece together five of the pieces before he got stuck and called up Erica. She walked into the Lab and stood regarding the table where Earl had collected all of the rock pieces. She picked up a few pieces and tried to join them up, but she couldn't. It was like trying to fit together a 3D jigsaw puzzle, some pieces looked like they went together until you tried to make them join up. Earl bought over a laptop and looked for the file of scanned images of the samples. Once he found that he simply asked a photographic program to join the pieces up if and wherever they could be joined. He watched as the program raced through a few hundred options before it rapidly showed the bulk of the pieces joining up to form a single block, one metre long and a third of a metre wide. It was ten centimetres thick. The image of the block, spun slowly on the screen, marred only by three missing pieces near the end of the block. Earl looked at Erica.

"Weird," he said,

"Jesus, the conspiracy nuts will go ballistic over this," Erica said.

"You know what it looks like," Earl said.

"Of course I know what it looks like, Earl," Erica said. "It looks like a frigging monolith. This is why Admin were getting all huffy about the black rocks to start with. Some smartass has planned this. I don't know how and I don't know why, but it is like those monoliths that kept appearing in weird places on Earth back in the twenties. Whoever did that, has managed to get one up here. Bloody clever, but still a pain the arse."

"I'll call Marley," Earl said.

*

"Admin are pissed off," Marley said.

"Admin are always pissed off," Earl said.

"Yeah, but now they are really pissed off. They've been ordered to find the missing parts," Marley said.

Erica turned to look at Marley. "When you say they've been ordered to find the missing pieces, you mean *we've* been ordered to find the missing bits," she said.

"Even if it is a hoax," Marley said, "they've been told they won't be getting any more contracts until it has been resolved. We are getting overtime. We are also getting some more crews assigned to us, as well as satellite support. They are throwing everything at this. Hoax or not, this is our priority for the foreseeable future." He turned to Earl. "Make up some grids and allocate them to the search teams. We'll concentrate on the place where Erica found the last piece and radiate out from there. I'll get Debs and her team to program the satellite searches. "

They found the three pieces after 8 months. The first one was close to where Erica had found her piece in the Mare Cognitum. This was the area that Marley's team shared with the Bounders headed by Luka Mills. Luka had reported a small geological anomaly only weeks after her team had been told to halt all other tests. The piece was found, bagged and transported via cart to the Dome. It was then months before the second missing piece was found.

Earl was used to getting far too many directives from admin and he tended to just skim read a lot of the mail from them. He saw the words Tycho Anomaly and sighed. The Tycho crater had been searched meticulously ever since eight pieces of the rock had been found there. In fact, the Tycho location was one of the reasons why hoaxers were long held responsible for the black rocks. The fact that the rock pieces were now a part of a compelling jigsaw puzzle, simply meant that the Tycho crater was once again a place of interest. Carts with geolink capabilities were meandering all across the crater. At first an onlooker would think the things were operating haphazardly, but Earl looked at the maps and he saw a very deliberate message was being "written" by the paths that the carts were taking. He punched in the stated parameters of the search vehicles just to make sure. He called Erica over to the screen.

"You know the carts that are geo-ing the Tycho crater?"

"Yes," said Erica. "What about them? Have they found something?"

"No, well not that I know. I just tracked their search patterns. Who programmed the search do you know?"

"Mills? I think it was Mills. Her Bounders Team got control of that area after they finished with Mare Cognitum. Why?"

Earll swung the screen around so that Erica could see the message that the search paths of the carts spelled out, or would spell out when they had completed their task.

"I'm sorry Dave, I'm afraid I can't do that," Erica read aloud. She looked confused. "Who is Dave?"

"Never mind. It's just Mills playing silly buggers. I'll tell them to knock it off."

Erica shrugged and walked off.

The carts trundled along. The satellites zipped silently overhead. The teams doing the searching and scanning had long since tired of it all. It was not easy trying to find a small piece of rock, on a very rocky world, covered in dust. The fact that the rock was black would have helped to make it stand out on the dusty grey surface of the moon, if every shadow on the moon was not equally as black. And, given the propensity of craters to create lots of ridges, there were a lot of shadowed areas on the moon. In the Tycho Crater the carts had been reprogrammed to wipe out the message they had created, however, in doing so, they found the second last piece of the black block.

"Marley carefully placed the newly found piece of the block into its position. It fell into place with a satisfying click.

"One to go," Marley said.

"Unless that one piece has been broken into smaller pieces," Earl said.

"God don't say that" Marley said.

"It could be worse than that," Erica said.

"How so?" Marley managed to look curious and very concerned at the same time.

"What if the last piece is indeed in small pieces, and, what if it is somewhere we haven't looked yet?" Erica asked. Just then Earl's laptop pinged. He went and looked at the screen.

"Admin," he said. "They want us to look on the dark side."

Marley looked at Erica as if this was her fault for even thinking about it.

They looked. Well, the satellites and scanners on carts looked. They even dragged out some old rovers to help in the search. They found some old Chinese and Russian landers and a few old satellites but nothing else. Admin asked them to collect the Landers just for interests' sake. There wasn't much the Russians could teach the rest of the world about space related topics but crashing hardware was one area they excelled in.

After a few months it was decided that they had looked everywhere possible in as much detail as possible, and it just wasn't going to happen. The monolith was going to have to remain incomplete, even though Erica wondered if this called into question actually naming it a monolith. No one wanted to engage with her on that topic and so she let it rest. Still, the whole enterprise seemed like a huge waste of time and resources.

*

Lisa Thripp read the memo detailing the scaling down of the monolith search. It was a shame as the new monolith had caught the attention of the public, and interest in NASA had grown again. As the CEO of NASA Lisa had been invited onto numerous talk shows and it had to said that she was a very capable performer. She also liked the attention very much.

She had grown into the role of chief Executive Officer of NASA from an early age. She had accompanied her father, astronaut Teddy Thrip on many publicity jaunts and, having completed numerous degrees in engineering and business management, she had landed a job in the administration of NASA, along with her father, who work in Human Resources. In fact, she had inherited his old office when he retired.

Lisa began writing a memo thanking all of the personnel on the moon and on Earth for their untiring efforts in trying to track down the last of the Tycho fragments as they were now called despite the fact that most of the rocks had not been located anywhere near the crater. Lisa was about to appear on an evening chat show, and she had dressed for the occasion. Her smart business suit was black, with some silver trim here and there. She thought it nicely matched the darkness of space and the sliver of the stars. She had been asked to bring along a few knick knacks or curios that the average viewer might be interested in, and she thought nothing would be better than a moonrock given that this whole recent episode had revolved around rocks on the moon. She hefted the black rock that her father said had come from the moon and thought it would do nicely. It was a rock, and it had the added personal touch of being something that her father had himself bought back from the moon. She stepped lightly through the door and pulled it shut behind her.

A moment later she came rushing back into the room, picked up her desk phone and madly began punching numbers into it.

*

There were twelve people around the table. Lisa Thripp sat near the windows. There were politicians, flight engineers, physicists and a philosopher. The chair of the meeting, General Andy Brown sat at the head of the table skimming through his tablet. He looked up suddenly and scanned the room.

"Is everyone here?"

People glanced around the table and then nodded.

"Ok, Let's begin," Brown said. "This shouldn't take long. We just need to decide the best thing to do with this rock." He sighed and tapped the table briefly. "First off, thanks to Dr. Thripp for finding the rock. We won't dwell on the circumstances of how a significant piece of lunar geology managed to get stored in an unrestricted storeroom, but there we go. Mistakes happen."

Lisa Thripp reddened slightly but people just put that down to disliking being the centre of attention. Others who knew her doubted that was the reason.

"We seem to have two options," Brown said. "We can either send this one up, or we can bring all of the others down." He sat back. "Your thoughts?"

One of the scientists pointed out that the facilities on earth were better suited to studying the monolith and they thought the lunar segments should be shipped to Earth. Two politicians agreed because they thought this would play well with their constituents. Another scientist wondered if there might be some danger attached to completing the monolith on Earth given the fact that the monolith was almost certainly of extra-terrestrial origin. The philosopher didn't think it would be of alien design, but he agreed that it would be safer if the study of the monolith were completed on the moon. The politicians agreed with this course of action because they thought it would play well with their constituents.

Lisa Thripp looked at each speaker with something approaching disdain.

"We are all aware," she began, and then paused. She didn't quite know how to approach this. "The umm, links to the more famous monolith...I'm talking about the science fictional monolith we all know about.... I mean...That was fiction. It wasn't real. It was a book."

"Technically it was a short story and then a film," one of the scientists said. "The famed Monolith was of course devised for the film version. Clark wrote the novelisation based upon the film."

"Well, whatever," Lisa said. "I still think it is just a hoax. A very good hoax, but a hoax none the less."

The meeting concluded with a motion to transport the rock back to the moon where extensive testing could be carried out in complete safety. This was communicated to the administrative teams at the moon base.

*

"Whose complete safety?" Erica asked.

"Not ours," Earl said. They were standing watching the base carts unload the supply ship. There were plastic packs of delicate instruments as well as crates of normal supplies.

"There's our coffee," Erica said, pointing to a large crate. "About bloody time."

They followed the train of carts into the base. A small group of techs and other staff escorted the Plastipaks into the relevant labs.

"So why this concern about safety?" Erica asked when they had forced open the crate containing their coffee.

Marley, drawn by the smell of coffee brewing, entered the kitchen. "They are worried that the monolith might do something as soon as we put it all together," he said in answer to Erica's question.

"Like what?" Erica asked.

"I've got no idea," Marley said. "Anyway, they are going to build a facility far away from the base and the reintegration process will proceed there."

"Reintegration process?"

"Putting all of the bits back together," Earl said.

"And it will all be done remotely, so no one will be in danger from anything that might happen," Marley concluded.

"I thought they were going to have a big meeting to decide whether to do that up here or down there," Erica said.

"They did," Marley said stirring his coffee. "They decided that up here would be best, safety wise."

"Oh well, that's me reassured," Erica said. "I notice they didn't include anyone from up here in the meeting."

Marley shrugged.

The Integration facility was built quickly. It was so far away from the moon base that anyone wanting to check on its progress had to refer to the screen that was dedicated to a round the clock broadcast. After the struts had been placed, the plastisheets covered the whole structure and the camera was moved inside. Erica glanced at the screen whenever she walked by it, but she wasn't motivated enough to download the "cast to her phone. A few people did and it became a fairly lively topic of conversation for a little while, but that soon passed. However, once the structure was complete and powered, the incomplete monolith was transported to the site. Then, people began to take notice. Erica assumed that the "cast was being sent to Earth because there had been an increase in journalists on the base and she and Earl were often batting away requests for interviews. And then, one morning, all of the staff were called in for a staff meeting.

Erica hated staff meetings as much as the next person and the next person was Earl who actually claimed he had a medically recognised aversion to them. He still had to attend them though. The staff gathered in Base Central, a large space that was opened up by moving some of the walls within the base. Admin types were all at the front of the space, presumably, Erica thought, because they either liked meetings or they needed to be seen at them. She noted the arrival of Miranda Kohl, the base commander. Once she moved to the centre of the small area cleared for speakers the whole room settled down.

She made a speech welcoming everyone and saying how it was a momentous day and how proud she was, and Erica found herself hoping against hope that this whole "monolith" thing was indeed a hoax and that nothing was going to happen. The more she thought about it, the weirder she thought the whole thing was. Why would anyone go to this much trouble to place a monolith on the moon? She knew that some had been placed in various locations on earth over the years and she just sort of assumed that this moon monolith was just an extension of that. Not that it made much sense to place the earth monoliths in hard to access locations either. And the thought that it might have been aliens was just dumb. After all, the whole idea of the monolith had been made up by Arthur C Clarke. Erica had seen the film!

Erica returned her attention to the speech being delivered by Miranda Kohl for a brief moment. She was talking about how it was a fantastic privilege to be working on the moon, and so, Erica reasoned that there was going to be another economy drive in the near future. After a bit more speechifying, Kohl managed to hand over the microphone to Stuart Sivens, the PR guru of the base. He flicked on the live feed from the Integration centre, and everyone settled to watch the screen.

Erica could see all of the pieces of the moon monolith laid out on a white plastic slab.

"Why have they separated it all up?" she asked Earl, who was beside her.

"Dramatic tension," he said.

They watched as small dogs, the automated all-purpose machines that were used to handle sensitive materials, fussed around the plastic slab, placing pieces of black rock into predetermined positions. The black monolith slowly took shape until only the last three fragments of the monolith remained.

"Do we know why our monolith was all over the place?" Erica asked. It was a question that hadn't occurred to her previously.

"Meteor strike probably," Earl said, without taking his eyes from the screen.

"Oh. Makes sense," Erica said.

One single "dog" placed two pieces into the monolith that was nearly complete on the slab. People moved and fiddled with things. And then, the last piece of the puzzle, the piece that had been shipped from Earth, was held over its place on the slab. There was a moment of silence, and then the piece was dropped into place with an audible "click".

There was silence.

Then all of the cracks that were in the monolith disappeared as it formed a solid whole.

Then all of the very finely tuned machines that were monitoring the monolith recorded something that forced every needle on all of the recording sensors to fly into the red. This was accompanied by an audible screeching sound that was picked up and broadcast by every speaker on the base. It was so loud that Erica actually slapped her hands to her head to block the noise.

"Jesus, what was that?" she said after the screech had died out.

"We are checking it out, "Earl said.

"Bloody hell," Erica banged the side of her head with her hand. "God, I think it cured my tinnitus!"

The tech crews that had been hanging around Kohl and the other admin heavies were all buzzing about various pieces of equipment. Erica could tell from the looks on their faces that none of them knew what had happened. In the meantime, Kohl was looking impatient and she clearly decided that she was only looking superfluous which is anathema to administrative people, so she purposefully walked off in the direction of her office as if some monumentally important task had been assigned to her.

*

Erica and Marley were discussing the problems they were having with the carts when Earl joined them.

Earl watched them fiddling around with the electronics of a cart for a few minutes.

"What's up with the cart?" he asked finally.

"Software problem," Marley said.

"It was that screech from the monolith," Erica said. "Everyone is reporting the same problem. It occurred just after that noise."

"How's your tinnitus? Didn't that go at the same time?"

"It's back, Erica said. "I hate it. If I could change one thing about me, that's the thing I'd change."

"You'd be spoilt for choice though," Earl said. he then added, "But seriously, I thought it was going to be your looks."

"Get stuffed," Erica said. "Tinnitus is no laughing matter. I used to think death would be good because I would get a break from this bloody ringing. Then I had a horrible thought..."

Earl looked up. Which was?"

"What if I didn't?"

"What do you mean? What if you didn't get relief from the tinnitus after you died?"

Erica nodded.

Earl looked concerned. "Yikes," he said. "That is a dark thought."

Marley wiped his hands after attempting to fix the cart.

"I think the electrics are shot," he said. "People have been having problems with all sorts of shit all over the base. We are going to need some serious amounts of spare parts sent up. When's the next shuttle?"

"There are two shuttles waiting to take the dignitaries back down so it's going to be a while before they get one loaded up to come back up here," Erica said. "And anyway, I doubt that they are going to be sending all those techs and scientist back until they've sorted out the monolith stuff."

The monolith "stuff" that needed sorting was identifying just what had occurred when the last piece of the monolith had been put in place. Clearly something had happened, and everyone was very keen to find out what. This was partly because the Russians and Chinese had deduced that the sound obviously ruined electronics and could therefore be used as a weapon against them, and partly because the Russians and Chinese wanted to find out how to use the sound as a weapon themselves. There was quite a delegation of Russian and Chinese techs and bureaucrats on the moon at present.

The first assessment of what had occurred indicated that a signal of some kind had been sent. No one knew what the signal meant, nor where it was sent, but it certainly seemed like a signal and that was therefore what was being investigated. Two facts pointed the investigators in this direction:

1. Someone had read the book by Arthur C Clarke and discovered that sending signals was what monoliths did.
2. The signal was tracked emanating from the moon and heading out into space by a variety of monitors who had been looking for just this sort of thing, but they were looking in another direction, so this signal surprised them somewhat.

Marley became the conduit for information that was promulgated in the various meetings that Admin were holding. He relayed the news to his crew, and they sat and discussed the latest findings, theories and guesses.

"So, it is definitely a signal. We know that for sure," Erica said. She was busy replacing mother boards in the carts that they had allocated. Earl and a few others were sitting around ripping old mother boards out of carts and cannibalising them for parts.

"But, if we don't know what it said, we don't know it was a message. Could have been random stuff." That was Ridley. He was one of those people who always took a contrary position to whatever was the dominant voice or thought in any discussion.

"Why would any intelligent being go to all this trouble to send random garbage to some unknown place in space," Patrice said.

"It isn't an unknown place in space," Earl said. "They traced it."

"How could they trace it?" Ridley asked. Erica noted that this wasn't a repudiation of the point that Earl made. Ridley just didn't have enough information to make a full-on smart-arse response just yet. That would come later.

"They had the originating point, which was here of course, and they had markers indicating that the message was directed to a certain point. It was a narrow cast, tight beam type of thing. It got picked up by deep space monitors, orbiters and other stuff. They have the coordinates but that isn't the really interesting part." Earl stopped talking as he levered a particularly tricky bit of electronics out of a cart. Everyone else just waited for him to finish what he was doing. Finally, Erica couldn't wait any longer.

"Ok, come on, tell us the interesting part then," Erica said.

"The interesting part was that the signal was directed at a specific place and time."

Ridley and Patrice looked at each other but neither felt comfortable about tackling this one.

"Space, *and* time?" Erica asked.

"Yep. It goes to a location about 59,220,000,000 k's away. And about sixty-two years ago.

Erica kept trying to jog the conversation along. "So, what's there?"

"Nothing," Earl said. It is empty space."

"Well did it just stop there?"

"Yeah, what happened to it," ridley asked. Did it just get tired?"

"It disappeared," Marley said.

"Erica frowned. "What do you mean? It can't have."

"Well, it didn't disappear as such because it wasn't visible to start with," Earl said. "But it went all wobbly and then couldn't be tracked."

"But" Marley said with the air of a man who is about to impart important information. "It did get picked up again. On Earth. That location is empty space now, but sixty-two years ago it is precisely where the Earth was located.

*

The sun blazed and the air was full of screeching, noisy birds. The palms were the only things moving and they weren't really moving much. They didn't so much indicate a breeze as highlight the fact that a breeze would have been welcomed. Arthur stepped up the stony path toward his front door. The heat made him long for the cool depths of the ocean and he promised himself a dive later in the day. Business first. The envelope bore a British stamp and Arthur stepped into the cooler interior of his house and kicked off his light sandals. The envelope also had the postmark of the main post office in Colombo, as well as a stamp from his local post office.

Arthur knew what it was before he pulled it out of the envelope. Took a knife and slit open the envelope. Among the papers he saw the title "The Sentinel" and sighed. They would need more that that old story of his, but he supposed it would be a good place to start. He did think it was odd that someone would send a copy of his own story to him all the way from England. He supposed they must think he didn't have any of his old stuff with him in Ceylon. He walked into the kitchen and flicked on the radio. Just as he did, the speaker of the radio emitted an electronic scream that made Arthur grab at his head in response. He squeezed his eyes shut against the screech and had a vague impression of a pink beam for a second and then it stopped.

"Bloody hell," Arthur said as he examined the speaker of the radio. He shook it and then turned the radio on again. Soft music played. Then a news report. He stopped for a moment and then he quickly walked into his study. He began typing notes.

Notes for Black Rock

This was the third story I wrote upon my return to writing. I realised that all of the stories I had written so far were set on Earth, or in a version of Earth in the case of *The Waiting Tree*. I decided I wanted to get off Earth as it were, and my first tentative step was onto the moon.

Again, I had no idea what I wanted to write about, and I just started writing. I had the first scene in my head, and I simply followed on from that. I didn't even have to do a lot of rewriting. I got quite excited when I had the idea of introducing Arthur C Clarke's monolith from *2001 A Space Odyssey* into the story, and even more excited when I thought of actually having Arthur C Clarke appear at the end. I thought this was really clever, but it has probably been done a thousand times. It was fun to write, and I was very pleased with it, but afterwards it did occur to me that if you had not read *2001 A Space Odyssey,* or if you had not seen the film, you might not really get what this story is about.

A Big Metal Cylinder

The ship was lying on a scrappy slope. Branches and broken trees and shrubs were bunched up on one side of the cylinder. It was a shiny grey metallic colour. There were no external features and if any had existed, Furness thought they had probably been broken off in the landing, if indeed there had been a "landing". The area looked like a crash site.

"And we have tried everything radio wise?" Furness said. His assistant was nervously standing beside him.

"Every frequency. Short wave long wave. We've done everything but bang on the side." Chandra regretted saying that as soon as he had said it. Furness had a reputation for getting results and this was going to be the biggest result anyone had ever had. Ever. In the history of everything.

"Well, we might not try that just yet," Furness said. There was a faint mechanical noise coming from the east. It would be another news chopper trying their luck. Furness noted the fact that the helicopter had already crossed the exclusion zone just by the sound of it. They had not actually shot down any of the many news aircraft that patrolled the limits of the exclusion zone, but Chandra felt that Furness wouldn't lose too much sleep over downing a chopper if it meant the others would stay away. Of greater concern were the many individual reporters, and UFO enthusiasts who kept trying to creep up on the site on foot. Fifteen had been taken away, flown interstate and imprisoned. Furness had suggested that they all remain deprived of access to news sources and the internet just to really hammer home the point. The chopper noise got quieter as the offending helicopter turned away from the exclusion zone. Furness imagined that there was a reporter on board going off his head and trying to convince the pilot to turn back.

Off to one side of the cylinder a group of comms experts were trying to decide ways to communicate with whoever, or whatever was in the cylinder. One of them wanted signs with the words 'Hello' and 'Peace' written in different languages, just in case whoever, or whatever was in the cylinder had been studying earth languages. Furness looked around. The army were prominent and many of them had guns trained on the ship, which pretty much negated the "Peace" sign idea. Other soldiers were busy positioning cannon and field artillery. The police were staking out higher ground behind the army positions. A fleet of ambulances were parked on an old fire access track. They were kept company by about twenty fire engines. The site was twenty kilometres inland, and Furness knew that there were three naval destroyers stationed off the coast.

The biggest contingent by far was from the state and federal governments. There were politicians and public servants from just about every department that could conceivably construe some sort of responsibility that linked it to the site. Furness had questioned the presence of officials from the Department of Finance, but he presumed someone had to pay for all of this, so it made sense.

"The government people are getting nervy," Chandra said. "They reckon that three weeks is an awful long time for whatever is in there to survive."

"I suppose we could shoot our way in," Furness said. "I mean, look around you. We have the firepower." Furness was beginning to think that the idea of banging on the side of the craft might be a good idea. The craft had crashed into the Victorian Highlands on September the 3rd. The first responders had arrived the next day and as soon as they realised what they were dealing with, they called in the army, and every other service they could think of, and that included the navy as one of the State Emergency Service officers had served in the navy.

Since then, the Americans, British and the French had all insisted that they look after the situation. To placate them they had each been allowed to send a delegation to the site. The Leader of the American contingent was late as he was currently trying to tie up some film deals with his contacts back in Hollywood. The French party had got caught up at the Melbourne International Film Festival by mistake. The English delegation was always busy doing interviews. Once they arrived on site, the French delegation had taken an active interest in the capsule, and they spent most of their time talking selfies in front of it, and taking measurements of everything around it.

*

A base office had been set up on the back of a semi-trailer. They had a separate mobile office for the tech crews, but this one was strictly for administration. Furness was sitting at the head of the table. "Ok," Furness said. "We are going to bang on the side of the capsule." There were looks around the table. Some thought that this was a great idea, and others thought it was a terrible idea given all of the technology that had been gathered at the site. The capsule had become the most watched object in history, and it was still a total mystery. The radar, Scans x-rays and other means of discovering what made a thing tick had all failed miserably. Apart from one small handheld recorder that had indeed discovered that the capsule did actually tick. So, tick yes, but what made it tick, not so much.

*

Furness was aware that the eyes of the world were upon him. Every step he took, and every move he made was recorded. He unconsciously began humming the Police song that came to mind. He knew it was safe to approach the capsule as no dangerous emissions had been recorded, along with everything else that was not being detected. He looked at Chandra. His assistant was covered in a safety suit that obscured his features. On his right, another assistant wore just plain old jeans and a check shirt. She looked back at Furness with a confident look. They stopped about four meters from the capsule. It looked solid enough. It was on a slight lean where the crushed trees beneath it had failed to support its weight. The capsule was about ten metres long. It looked like a carriage from the London underground, shaped as if it needed to fit into a tunnel.

Furness looked at both of the suited-up assistants who both nodded. He ignored the pleas for situational reports constantly being made from the people at the edge of the inner exclusion zone, and he walked quietly up to the cylinder. He listened intently. There was a tick. It was hard to determine whether it was just the metal contracting or expanding, or if it was from movement as the weight of the cylinder crushed a bit more tree. He was counting seconds in his mind until the next tick. It came two minutes later. Pretty much the same rate as had been reported earlier. He raised his clenched fist. He hesitated for no apparent reason. They had decided that a firm double rap on the cylinder would be the best approach. A soft rap might not be heard inside, and a real whack with a hammer that had been suggested, might be construed as an attack. It had also been suggested that, after a prudent wait of say, a minute or so, a second double rap should then be applied to the cylinder. Furness leaned forward and rapped upon the metal. Before he could apply the second of the double rap, the cylinder disappeared.

Furness was left standing with his hand raised having applied the second rap to nothing. He looked toward his assistants. Chandra was looking at his hand-held detector.

"Nothing" Chandra said.

"I can see that," Furness said. "Where did it go?"

The other assistant was advancing slowly with her hands outstretched, trying to feel the presence of the cylinder.

"It's not here anymore," she offered at last.

Furness sighed. "I can see that too," he said. "Or rather, can't. You know what I mean." There was a clamouring on his earpiece as many voices tried to ask him the same question in twenty different ways. He had lost the most important artifact ever to be found on Earth. He was not having a good day.

*

Retirement suited Furness. He had long cultivated a solitary life. He had few friends, even fewer relatives and that was fine by him. His modest unit was on the edge of the retirement village. The various social clubs had long since given up trying to coax him into joining in with activities, and he was generally regarded by all as 'a bit of a loner', or by the more prosaic, 'a moody, grumpy old bastard'. He did deign to play golf with a couple of other ex-coppers, but only because he was bad at it, and he could honestly say that his lack of ability meant that he spent the time on the course pretty much alone as he negotiated the rough, or, if he was feeling particularly grumpy, the very rough on the next fairway. He was on the golf course when the helicopter arrived. Like the others he looked up at the sound of the approaching chopper thinking maybe some poor bastard had suffered a heart attack on the course. He grew alarmed when the helicopter looked like it was landing on the fairway he was on. This could mean that one of his group might have had the medical emergency. He didn't particularly like the people he was playing with, but he didn't wish them that sort of handicap. He watched as the chopper landed. He watched as three people emerged from the chopper. He watched as they ran toward him. He turned around to see who was injured behind him, and turned around again just in time to see them bundle him up and carry him to the chopper. He shouted his protests until a headset was clapped on his head.

"What the fuck do you think you are doing?" he shouted into the mic attached to the headset. He was about to add, "Do you know who I am?" when he realised that they would know precisely who he was. It also meant he knew why they were adducting him.

"That fucking cylinder is back again, isn't it?"

A crackling voice came back on his headset. "Can't talk about it Sir. Sorry about the intrusion, but it is urgent. We've got a flight of about three hours. There are sandwiches and a drink in that bag."

The flight took only two hours and twenty minutes. He recognised the area, but then, all of the high-country bush looked pretty similar. Hills that were once mountains that had been weathered down over the millennia, a thick coverage of eucalypts and tee tree, all with that scrabbly, blue-green roughness. A glaring patch had been carved out of the vegetation and the chopper was clearly heading toward it. As they got closer, Furness could see army supply vehicles, as well as earth movers stationed underneath the trees off to one side of the clearing. Off to the other side were tents and caravans.

Furness was led into a large caravan. There were a two army officers, two well-dressed suited men and a well-dressed woman, and two people in overalls. The well-dressed woman smiled and indicated a chair.

"You probably know why you are here," she said. "I'm Marion Wood. I've been invited to oversee this operation, and I've been given carte blanche to recruit anyone I think may be of use. As you noted in the chopper, this is indeed about 'that fucking cylinder' as you accurately named it. It is back."

Furness recognised bureaucracy when he saw it and he knew it was pointless to complain about it. But he did anyway. "It is hardly "recruitment" when one is abducted from one's game of golf. Without explanation," he added.

"True, and you have our most sincere apologies, but let's face it, you don't even like golf, or the people you were playing with."

"Not the point," Furness said petulantly. "So where is it?"

The woman leaned forward in her chair and activated a screen on the wall. "It is exactly where it was last time. I should point out that you are still bound by the secrecy agreement you signed when you were on this case years ago."

"Same place?" Furness said, somewhat redundantly. The woman nodded.

"Exactly the same place?"

The woman nodded but it was a different nod this time. This nod was aimed at one of her assistants and it was clearly an instruction. The screen on the wall split into two screens. They seemed identical. They showed the cylinder lying amongst the wreckage of native bushland. It was at exactly the same angle as far as Furness could tell.

"These two shots are twenty years apart," Marion Wood said. Furness stood and examined the images closely. "Wow," he said finally.

"There is one other thing," Marion said. "The cylinder knocked back."

Shortly after the cylinder had reappeared, various detecting devices recorded two distinct knocks from the area. A preliminary response team found the cylinder and soon after that, every agency that had attended the scene on its previous visit, had shown up again. Each agency had new equipment they were keen to test out, and again, there was a fair bit of competition to get the best locations near the cylinder.

"This is going to be a slow conversation if all we get is a reply to our initial knock twenty years after the event," Furness said. "I probably won't be around for the next one. Although, I have to say, I'm not really sure why I am here for this one."

"Well, we've knocked. Many times. At least when you knocked you got a response."

"The thing disappeared," Furness said.

"True, but that at least was a response. We get nothing. So, we want you to knock again."

*

A group of people trekked out to the site. After just five minutes of walking, they were drenched in sweat.

"Bloody weather," Marion observed. "Is it always this humid?"

"No," Furness said. "Sometimes it's worse. Climate change. It was never this bad years ago."

As they walked, Furness and Wood debated the reason for the disappearance of the cylinder and an aide kept taking notes of everything they said. In fact, two aides took notes, but they only knew about the first one.

"We don't think it disappeared so much as went to another time," Wood said. "We think they or it, experience time in a different manner."

"How so? What makes you think that?"

"Their response. It wasn't really a knocking sound. It was a long-drawn-out sound, but when played at a higher speed, it sounds exactly like the sound it made when you knocked on it. So, we think they operate on a different state of time. That and the really long delay after you touched it and it disappeared, until now."

"That's not exactly definitive, is it?" Furness said. "Has any work been done on the suspected purpose of the thing? Someone said you are using morse codes to communicate with it?"

"We've used the language signs that were suggested last time," Wood said. "But we have concentrated on morse. If knocking is the best we can hope for, we should prepare for it. As to purpose who knows?"

"True," Furness said. "I mean their knock might have said anything. For all we know it's a monitoring device set to record when this atmosphere is suitable for invading aliens."

"Where did that come from?" Wood asked.

"It was just one of thousands of explanations we got from our experts last time.

The aides took notes.

Whilst it was true that there were hardly any newspapers left, the same cannot be said about headlines. A story appeared the next day in all of the reputable online news outlets; "Alien Sensor Alerts Space Monsters," the headlines screamed metaphorically. "Invasion Imminent?" they then queried. The non reputable online news outlets went with "Alien Probe signals to Monster Invasion Force!!!" Although not all of them adopted the use of multiple exclamation marks.

"How could they quote me?" Furness asked. "I didn't say that!"

"You did," Marion said. "Actually, what you said was, "For all we know it's a monitoring device set to record when this atmosphere is suitable for invading aliens" end quote. They just left off the "for all we know" bit. It was one of the aides. Well, it was a reporter pretending to be an aide. He has been carted offsite. We'll deal with him later. For the moment we have bigger problems."

"They spelt my name wrong," said Furness. "Furmness." He spelt it out. "Sorry, what other problems?"

"Well now we have the world's attention again. We were hoping to keep it quiet. We have already had to have the army warn media choppers off with shots across their bow, or whatever helicopters have at the front. There is a queue five k's long of media vans. Every satellite that could be moved to cover us is now covering us. If you look up and smile it will be on every news site around the world and on YouTube." She paused as if to catch her breath and Furness was worried that the list was going to continue. "In short," she said, "We are the world's biggest story right now. And for the foreseeable future."

"If we just stay quiet, maybe they will lose interest and go away," one of the suits said. Marion looked down and saw the aide was taking notes. The aide saw that she saw he was taking notes. "It wasn't me, ma'am," he said. "I only just arrived."

"Where are you from?" Marion asked.

"Here," the aide said. "I was born in Australia."

"I meant what department are you from?" Marion said icily.

"Sorry. Finance," he said.

"Ok you can stay. No more notes." She turned to Furness. "I think we need a response from the cylinder. Something chipper. Something upbeat. Something positive and non-threatening."

"You want a "chipper" response from an alien artifact that is behaving in a weird manner, that possibly experiences time in a totally alien way and that disappeared the last time we tried anything?"

"If it isn't too much trouble," Marion said. "And if you could manage it by later this afternoon, that would be terrific. Now, I have a huge press conference to conduct." She smiled and walked away with the aide from Finance.

"I'll need some staff," Furness shouted as she walked away.

"You have me," a voice said behind him. He turned and saw Chandra, his old assistant. For a moment Furness was speechless.

"Chandra! This is amazing!" He took the man by the shoulders and hugged him. Then he pulled back again. "I don't believe it! You have hardly aged a day!" Furness was wondering if proximity to the capsule had an effect on the aging process. He knew Chandra had stayed with the project for some time after the cylinder disappeared. Maybe there was a residual "anti-aging" field still in place.

"I'm Derrick, Chandra's son. Dad died a few years ago."

"Oh," Furness said. "I'm sorry. He was a good man."

"Yep," said Derrick and there didn't seem to be anything to add to that.

Furness and Derrick watched Marion's press conference together. It was hard to tell just how many journalists were in attendance as the camera stayed fixed upon an empty podium, but the general static of background noise made it clear that there were a lot of people crammed into the room. Furness didn't even know where the event was taking place. He didn't recall any rooms this big anywhere near the cylinder site. It must be in the nearest city. Then Marion strode to the podium. A line of serious looking people shuffled into position behind her, presumably to nod sagely when required.

"Good afternoon, ladies and gentlemen. Here is how this is going to work. I am going to read a short statement. I will then take ten questions from the floor, and I promise to answer as fully as I can. Then I will be leaving. Lots to do as I am sure you will understand." She paused for a moment to indicate the prepared statement was about to begin.

She spoke about the history of the site. How the cylinder had been discovered. What attempts had been made to ascertain its origins and purpose. She spoke about the reasons why the existence of the cylinder was kept from the public. She spoke about how successive governments had agreed to keep the information secret. She spoke about the role of the United Nations in these deliberations, and she also detailed everything they knew about the cylinder which, apart from basic things like measurements, was not a lot. She talked about Furness and how it was decided that he would be the one to lead the examination of the cylinder and she spoke about how he had bravely attempted actual physical communication with the cylinder. And then she discussed how it had disappeared, and now reappeared. Then she paused and one eager young reporter tried to jump in with the first question, but Marion held up her hand.

"I would now like to address the plainly dangerous and inaccurate reporting of certain comments that were garnered from a private conversation and were then taken out of context. These comments stated that it was a fact that the cylinder is some sort of device that will alert some random alien species that the Earth is ripe for invasion. Now before someone states that these words were indeed stated by an official, I would like to put it into context. The official said, and I quote, "For all we know it's a monitoring device set to record when this atmosphere is suitable for invading aliens." End quote. Now, an irresponsible journalist, took those words, left out the "for all we know" bit and went ahead with the story." Despite her using her very best stern voice, Marion felt that she was not quite cutting through with her audience. They seemed distracted. It was as if they had to sit through her little speech before they got to spring a surprise of their own. She turned around to look at her entourage and they all seemed suitably serious and approving of her message. They nodded enthusiastically when they saw her looking at them. She turned back to the crowded room.

"Ok. Questions." Hundreds of hands went up and a few started gabbling questions. She picked out a friendly looking man to her right.

"Is there any official reaction to the fact that this cylinder has been appearing in the same place, every twenty years, for at least a hundred years that we know of?"

"I shall have to get back to you on that one," Marion said. "No more questions." She rushed off the stage.

Furness watched the live feed of Marion Woods questioning her staff. Basically, this meant watching her scream obscenities punctuated by references to incompetence, laziness, poor research and a set of historical photographs and old news reports that did indeed show that the cylinder had been either reappearing every twenty years, or, it had been in the one place for over a hundred years. However, subsequent research did prove that it was not always present at the site. Furness knew that the result of the leak about the quote and the stuff up over the timeline would result in only one course of action for the project.

Security was stepped up. This basically meant Furness had to show his pass a lot more often. He was standing in the exact same place as he was twenty years previously. This had been verified by checking the vision from all of the cameras used before. Once again, he stood with his hand raised, ready to make one small rap for mankind and it wouldn't be a rap this time anyway, so Furness decided not to use that line much to Marion Woods displeasure. She had thought of it after all.

An international group of linguists, philosophers and diplomats had met and deliberated for days on what message they should send. Furness took the small piece of paper from his pocket and at the appointed time, began to run his hand slowly across the surface of the capsule.

He then slowly wrote the morse code for each letter of the message they had decided to send with a long stroke of his hand for a dash and a short stroke of his hand for a dot.

Dash Dash Dot

Dot dash dot

Dot

Dot

Dash

Dot dot

Dash dot

Dash dash dot

Dot dot dot

He felt a little let down. He thought that all of the world's best minds might have come up with something a bit better than "Greetings".

His disappointment was short lived, however. Just five minutes after Furness had completed his message, the cylinder began to reply.

The tension on site was intense. Everyone was either straining to hear the long slow noises emitting from the capsule, or they were trying to see the screen that was showing the slow morse code response as real letters. The entire response took four hours and fifteen minutes.

The message was:

"This is an automated message. Please do not respond to this message. This sensor measures the atmosphere of this planet in order to gauge its suitability for colonisation."

Furness looked at the screen which showed Marion Wood via Zoom. He had wondered what aghast actually looked like and now he knew.

There was a ping from the cylinder. Furness had the awful feeling that inside the machine, a little red light had just turned green.

Notes for Big Metal Cylinder

I started this one with just the image of a large metal cylinder lying in the remote bush near my home. I just liked the idea of a very alien looking artifact sitting in the middle of the Australian bush. The story just grew around that one idea. I like stories that explore a fairly simple idea, that then spiral off into something far more significant at the end of the story. Maybe I should write more about that more significant 'post story' idea, but then I wouldn't have that myriad of possibilities that exists at the end of the story.

The Australian bush, for those of you who do not know it, is quite capable of having objects like the Big Metal Cylinder, just lie around undisturbed for ages. Sometimes, when you stand on a hill in the middle of the bush neat where I live, you can imagine all sort of wonderful things being hidden by the seemingly endless bush. Many aircraft have gone missing in the wilds of Australia and despite extensive searches, they are never found. Many people, sadly have also gone missing and are never seen again. It is considered something of a miracle if a missing person is found alive after getting lost in the bush.

Some of the People, Some of the Time

1947

It was summer, in early July in Roswell. Abe Shaw was studying the night sky when he saw a strange light moving North at quite a speed. Later, Shaw was adamant that he really did see the lights, as he only got hallucinations when he was drinking vodka, and he was sticking strictly to bourbon on the night in question. Or it might have been whiskey, as he had recently celebrated a significant birthday, and he had been given a nice bottle of single malt. Or brandy. It didn't matter. Shaw was pretty sure he had seen the lights. Or light. It had been green, then it changed to a sort of orangey colour, and then it turned red. Shaw believed that this series of colour changes were perhaps linked to the speed of the "flying machine". He decided the best thing to do was to follow the lights in order to discover more about them. There had been reports of various phenomena in the skies over New Mexico for some time and Shaw thought he might be able to make a few bucks out of the sighting. He jumped into his truck, floored the accelerator and raced through a set of experimental traffic lights being trialled on the outskirts of Roswell. He was pulled over and taken into custody.

Only minutes later, Jean and Eddy O'Meara saw what they described as a "big, whooshing thing" that passed right over their car and displayed a range of flashing lights.

Jean O'Meara – My Eddy was just pulled over on the side of the road. He said his glasses needed cleaning and he was doing that with one of those new magic cloths that gets rid of all the grime that you get on glasses. I would have cleaned mine too, but I had left them at home. Eddy only wears his glasses for reading and driving and seeing things. These lights came a whizzing from behind us and they went clear over us and kept on a going. They was heading towards Roswell.

Reporter – Was there any noise?

Jean O'Meara – You mean like strange engine sounds? Or weird musical notes? Or like the sound of rushing air? Or just a strange eerie whistling noise? You mean like that?

Reporter – Yes, just like that!

Jearn O'Meara No.

Reporter – Oh. I thought you said there was a "whooshing" sound?

Jean O'Meara – Did I? I sometimes have trouble with words. Oh! We did hear a police car go by, chasing old Abe Shaw's truck! Is that useful?

*

There was a crumpled mess of fabric, cords and some metallic parts lying in the middle of a hanger. The air was warm. Captain Shaffer had wished they could open the hanger doors and let in a bit of a breeze, but he had been told to keep everything as it was until General Liddet had arrived. Shaffer looked at the tangled cords and fabric. He had an overwhelming urge to rearrange a part of the fabric to make it look a bit more symmetrical, but he was able to control the urge.

Behind a screen erected by some of the Military Police there was a lot of activity. Lights moved around, there were flashes from cameras and underlying it all there were hushed discussions. Shaffer wanted to be a part of those discussions, but he had been ordered to look after the pile of junk he was guarding. There was a creak of metal and Shafer looked over to see General Liddet walking through doorway towards him.

The General marched up to the pile of debris and regarded it for a moment. Shaffer had not met the General before and he was a little surprised at how closely he resembled how Shaffer had pictured him. He was rotund, red faced and had a jowly, sweaty face. His uniform looked like it had been applied rather than put on. The General pointed to the pile before him.

"That's a weather balloon. I've never seen a weather balloon before, and I know it is a weather balloon." He turned to Captain Shaffer as if it was impossible for him to swivel his neck. "Why am I being shown a weather balloon?"

"This was the material the farmer, Mr. Bezel, delivered, Sir" Shaffer said. "He said he saw lights in the sky, followed where they had been heading and found this." Shaffer pointed to the broken weather balloon for emphasis.

"What in God's name made him think this was some sort of spaceship from out of space?"

"I don't know Sir."

"So where is the flyer saucer I was told about?" The General stood turning his whole body left and right.

"Just over there, Sir. Behind the screen." Shaffer pointed again.

General Liddet strode away, and Shaffer followed him. A couple of guards saluted and pulled the screen to one side so the General could enter the area. For a moment Shaffer thought they were going to slide the screen back into place without allowing him to follow the General, but they just assumed that he was a part of the General's entourage.

The flying saucer wasn't in much better shape than the weather balloon. It was about ten metres long, and it tapered at each end. One end, and Shaffer assumed that this was the front of the craft, had been badly damaged in the crash. The entire craft was a uniform silvery grey colour and there was a faint chemical smell emanating from it.

General Liddet walked slowly around the craft. At one point he gently kicked the metal hull. There was a dull, echoey thud. He bent and peered into what looked like a window.

"Crew?" he asked.

One of the MP's stepped forward. "Autopsy, Sir."

The General made a sort of derisory sound. "I think we know how they died," he said. "But I guess they will be doing all sorts of tests and whatnot. Who are all these people?" The General didn't indicate which people, but Shaffer thought he must be referring to the photographers and staff making notes.

"They've all been vetted Sir," Shaffer said, "All a part of the investigation."

"How come the farmer only brought in the remains of the weather balloon and not this? I mean this at least looks like a space machine. Is he an idiot or something?"

Shaffer and the MP looked at each other as if deciding who needed to be the one to speak. Finally, Shaffer said, "He didn't find this Sir. He saw the lights, found the weather balloon and thought that was odd, and didn't look any further. We sent out a team to look around and they found this." The was a period of silence. Shaffer once again looked toward the MP who gave a little shrug in return. The silence continued until at last the General turned around to look at Shaffer.

"How many?"

Shaffer was confused.

"Crew Sir?"

"No. How many people went out in the team that found this. Who else knows about the Spaceship?" After a very brief pause, he added, "And how many Crew on the ship?"

"Eight on the team Sir," the MP said. "And two crew, that we know of. Sir. All good men Sir. Reliable."

"The crew?" the General asked.

"Um. The men Sir."

Shaffer decided it was a good time to ask what he should do about the press queries he was getting. "What do we do about the press Sir?"

"Well, if it were up to me, I'd shoot half of them, damned commies." Shaffer must have looked confused again.

"Oh, did you mean generally, or were you wondering what we should do about them in a specific case?"

"Specifically about this Sir. I mean it is the story of the century, and we are going to be swamped with press."

"This is the military son. You just deny everything."

1957

Shaffer was seated outside an office in the White House. He had heard that many people who get called into a meeting in the White House are seated in an area that is meant to intimidate them before they actually go into the meeting. Shaffer was seated opposite a fish tank. He worried that this meant that people thought he was easily intimidated. Perhaps they wanted to imply he had a short attention span, like a goldfish. Then he chided himself for being so paranoid. He looked closely at the fish. Were they guppies? He didn't know anything about fish. Were guppies considered pretty powerful in the world of fish? He doubted it. Guppy. It didn't sound like something powerful. He looked to his right and saw two burly men in overalls walking toward him. They slowed as they got to him and Shaffer began to feel more mind games clamouring for his attention. The two men picked up the fish tank and gently carried it away.

A woman came out of a door that Shaffer hadn't noticed.

"Colonel Shaffer? Do step this way."

Shaffer stood and followed the woman. The room he walked into was filled with a large wooden table; He recognised General Liddet, but everyone else seemed to be civilians. The woman who ushered him in, left via another door on the other side of the room.

"Ah Colonel Shaffer." The speaker was seated at the head of the table. "We are not standing on ceremony here so don't feel the need to salute. I am General White. You don't need to know the names of the other people here although you do know General Liddet." Shaffer nodded at Liddet who simply nodded in reply.

"We are a cross-service committee looking into the incident at Roswell in 1947." General White rifled through some papers, paused and then indicated a seat that was vacant. "Please do sit Colonel Shaffer." Shaffer sat. He looked around the room. It was painted in pastel colours and there were no windows. There were eight people seated around the table. Shaffer was sure that two men were from the FBI. He was surprised they were not wearing sunglasses. They seemed to be completely indifferent to the deliberations of the committee which pretty well sealed the FBI connection as far as Shaffer thought. The rest of the people were either Navy or Marines, but two were definitely Air Force. They sat happily sipping coffee and eating pastries.

"Now then," White said at last. "We are getting a lot of flak about the "incident" at Roswell. It turns out that people have been investigating the phenomena that allegedly occurred that night, and people are simply not buying into our blanket denial that anything occurred."

"Thin end of the wedge," Liddet said. "You start entering into a discussion about anything military and pretty soon you will have every wannabe reporter questioning pretty much every decision ever made by the people best equipped to know what in fact they are doing and what the circumstances are, pertaining to the situational parameters extant at the time of the decisions being promulgated both within and outside the operating, er, things that they are doing at the time."

"Quite," said General White. "So we need to adopt a different narrative Vis a Vis "the story"."

"That's not what I said," said General Liddet.

"Nevertheless. Colonel Shaffer, you were in charge of the remains of the weather balloon on the night in question were you not?"

"Well, I'm not sure I was "in charge" of anything. I was detailed to show the remains to General Liddet when he arrived."

"No need for false modesty Colonel. Now, the farmer who recovered the remains of the weather balloon was of the opinion that the remains actually constituted some form of extra-terrestrial vehicle or mode of transport did he not?"

"Well yes he did, but..."

"In fact, he actually signed a statement to that effect, didn't he?"

"Yes." Shaffer said, pleased that that he was able to answer a question emphatically.

"You conducted the interview with," and here he consulted some notes, "Farmer Mack Brazel."

The discussion ebbed and flowed, but Shaffer got the distinct impression that the meeting was really just a formality. The decision to put out the story about the "event" being nothing more than an errant weather balloon had already been made and this exercise was simply so that some administrators could ensure that they had covered their tracks... Or their asses. At the end of the meeting everyone signed some papers to guarantee that secrecy and Shaffer wandered out of the White House still wondering why he had been invited to the meeting in the first place.

1967

Senate inquiry into the alleged cover up of military operations, Roswell 1947. Present – Sen J Curtis (Rep Georgia), Sen. M. Comben (Rep, Montana), Sen. G. Clarkson (Dem. California) and H. Shaffer (Colonel ret).

Sen. Curtis – Mr Shaffer you are aware of the cover up that took place during and after the event that took place at Roswell in 1947?

Shaffer – Um. No?

Sen. Clarkson – Is that a question Mr. Shaffer? Are you asking us if we knew if you were aware of the cover up?

Shaffer – Umm. No... No. I mean. What cover up? I guess that means I was not aware of the cover up given that I didn't know there was a cover up.

Sen. Curtis – Mr. Shaffer did you or did you not attend a meeting held in the White House on March 4, 1957, where it was decided that the American people would be lied to about the events surrounding the alleged sighting of what has come to be known as an Unidentified flying Object.

Shaffer – I did attend a meeting yes.

Senator Curtis – And you raised the idea of attributing the strange events of that night in Roswell to what was referred to as (checks notes) and I quote, "an errant weather balloon" end quote.

Shaffer – I didn't raise the idea. But that was what was decided upon.

Sen. Clarkson – By you.

Shaffer – Well, I think I agreed.

Sen Clarkson – You agreed...

Shaffer – That was the mood of the meeting.

Sen Clarkson – Who was at that meeting, Mr. Shaffer?

Shaffer – Besides me? Um... I recall General Howard Liddet being there. I don't know the names of any other attendees.

Sen Curtis – So you and the late General Liddet.

Sen. Clarkson – What was General Liddet's position?

Shaffer – I think he said he wanted to just keep denying anything happened. He said that was the way the military always did things.

Sen. Curtis – But you thought otherwise.

Shaffer – I don't think so...

Sen. Clarkson – Mr. Shaffer is this your signature on an interview where you suggest to Mr. W. Brazel, the farmer who found the weather balloon debris, that it could well have been part of some sort of extra-terrestrial ship?

Shaffer – I think I made a joke about something like that.

Sen. Curtis – Very good Mr. Shaffer. That will be all. You may go. Shaffer leaves.

Sen Comben – All well and good. We can put out a press release blaming Shaffer for lying to the public about the whole thing being a damned weather balloon. As if anyone was going to believe that load of horse hockey.

Sen. Clarkson – It still leaves us with the problem of what we tell people now.

Sen. Curtis – Do we need to tell them anything? I mean old Liddet was a curmudgeon, but he was right about keeping military issues out of the public domain.

Sen. Comben – These are different times my friend.

Sen. Clarkson – Well we might as well just do what we usually do.

Sen. Curtis – Blame the Ruskies?

Sen. Clarkson – That's an option, but we could be a bit more subtle about it. We could say that it was a secret weapon for use *against* the Russians. That way, it is all kept secret and anyone who gets too close can be locked up for Treason.

Sen. Comben – It sounds like the way to go.

1977

"The story about the anti-Russian weapon just isn't going to cut it any longer General."

General Fisher looked at the two young men. They were wearing suits. He didn't like dealing with suits. He liked uniforms. Uniforms did what they were told.

"Listen son," Fisher said wearily. "I don't much care what is going to cut it or not cut it. Now I know you folk down at the FBI are getting all jittery over all of these rumours. Why we didn't just stick with a denial beats me. Trust me, nothing beats a flat denial and then silence. We laid the foundations for the denial back in "47 and even when that idea fell over, all you had to do was keep going with the balloon story. Ok, it wasn't the best story, but it did have the positive of being based on a part of the truth. And now you want to drop the anti Russkie weapon idea. Can't you just stick to one idea? Hell, by all means sound exasperated by all of these Unidentified flying Object stories, but don't tell the public the truth.

Agent Garner had heard that Fisher could be "difficult". Both he and Agent Georgeson had read transcripts of everything that occurred in Roswell in 1947. Sadly, it seemed that someone had leaked some of the intelligence gathered on that operation, and now there were all sorts of people claiming that there was a cover up. And that this had been followed by another cover up. The team tasked with looking into Roswell had decided it was time to shift the narrative.

"No one believes the Anti-Russian Weapon story," Garner said. "And the weather balloon story has been pretty well shot down. We just think that it would be a good idea to put out an alternate set of facts to put everyone's minds at ease."

"It don't matter if people believe it or not son," Fisher said. "We told them it was a weather balloon. We *showed* them it was a weather balloon. I mean, thems solid hard facts right there! Same with the weapon idea. I don't know who came up with that one, but it was a doozy. Cold war...Reds under the beds...What could be more patriotic than to believe a lie about a weapon to fight the commie Russians?"

"Nevertheless, we want to deliver another set of facts. It will keep people off our back and allow our teams to keep working on the ah... off world technology."

The General pushed back on his chair. He regarded the two agents coldly. He knew he couldn't order them to do or not do anything. If they outranked him that would be different. Fisher didn't mind following orders. He just didn't like civilians. He didn't care that Garner and Georgeson were from the FBI. He did care that they weren't military. He was actually physically uncomfortable with the fact that these two were free to ignore him.

"Ok. What are you going to go with?"

"We are going to say that what was found at Roswell was in fact a top-secret weapon that was being used *against* us, by the Russians," Garner said.

"And we shot it down," Georgeson added.

Fisher found himself impressed.

"It allows us to simply state that we cannot divulge any further information than that." Garner added.

Fisher smiled and nodded his head. "Because it is top secret. And any further queries could be construed as a serious breach of government protocols." Fisher paused for a moment weighing up the idea in his mind. "I like it. And of course, there is the added bonus that we shot down one of those commie bastards flying machines!"

"Plus, it allows for any further leaks of information that was gained on the night or subsequently," Garner added. "We can say other stories about the events were a disinformation campaign designed to catch the Russians off guard."

"And it also covers any of the information or technology that we have been able to glean form the crash vehicle subsequently,

"Hell son, even I don't know what we found out subsequently."

"We know," Garner said. "Anyway, we are just informing the military of our decision out of professional courtesy." Garner smiled and then both he and Georgeson exited the office.

General Fisher stood and faced his wall map. He always cheered himself up by identifying the current war zones and police actions around the world.

1987

Garner stood looking out of the window of his office. He watched the young agents and office staff parking their cars and mingling with each other as they entered the building. His intercom buzzed.

"Yes Claire?"

"Agent Davies is here Sir."

"Send him in," Garner said. He cleared some paperwork from his desk and got out his notebook and a pen. It was his habit to take notes whenever he was in a meeting no matter how small the meeting was, nor how unimportant the attendees were. In this case the only other attendee was Harley Davies. He was a young, black agent who had impressed with his work ethic and who was clearly on the up.

Davies entered and stood stiffly to attention as Garner finished fussing with his pen that was not working.

"Damn it," Garner said. "You would think that a nation that could put a man on the moon... well allegedly at least, could come up with a pen that worked. Have a seat Davies. Now then...This is a Roswell thing I take it."

"Yes Sir. Well not the actual incident Sir, more the aftermath."

There was a pause as Davies waited for a response from Garner, and Garner waited for Davies to keep talking. Garner gave the younger man a slight nod as if to encourage him to go on with what he wanted to say.

"Apparently some photographs have been circulating that purport to show the aliens from the craft in question. They are very convincing photographs Sir." Davies reached into a manila folder he was holding and withdrew three photographs. He placed them onto to the table in front of Garner.

"Wow, these are good," Garner said. He picked up the photographs and looked at them one after the other, and then placed them back on the table. "If they are fakes, they are very good ones."

"They aren't fakes Sir. We have identified them as a part of the original case photographs. Someone has leaked them. We do not know who leaked them, or when they were leaked. I mean, it is possible that someone stole them at the time and have just been holding onto them."

"And what action has been taken Agent Davies?"

"We are currently interviewing everyone who would have had access to the photographs either at the time or subsequently. As you know the security around this project has been extraordinarily tight, but that was not the case at the time of the incident. We know that there were reporters and press photographers around the site at the time and there were even some civilians nearby. Investigations are continuing, Sir."

Garner pushed the photos back toward Davies. "Obviously we are going to need a new story to explain this," Garner said.

"Perhaps not a new story Sir. We just need to embellish the existing story."

"Explain."

"Well, Sir, our current line is that the craft we captured was a Russian asset that was being used against the United States. No one has mentioned the fact that it was a manned craft up until now, and we have already put the confidentiality clause in place. All we need to do is add the fact that the Russians actually had used a manned craft on what was essentially a suicide mission."

"Well yes... All well and good," Garner said, "Apart from the fact that these..." and here he pointed the photographs, are clearly very small individuals. They are the size of children."

"Yes Sir." Davies stood up straight and as if about to announce something of major import. "It looks like those damned Russians have been using children in their evil war against democracy," he said.

"I like it Davies... And the fact that they are clearly, not human?"

"Experimental genetic engineering, Sir. Probably carried out by Nazis, in the employ of the Russians."

"Works for me," Garner said.

1997

The trade delegation was allocated rooms in one of Moscow's best hotels. The delegates simply assumed that every room they were in would be bugged and behaved accordingly. The only problem was that this meant that any pre meeting planning would need to be carried out in the Revolution Square that was opposite the Hotel Metropol. The four main members of the trade delegation were deep in conversation when their guide Dimitry, found them and advised that due to an administrative error, the members of the Ministry of Natural Resources and Environment and the Ministry of Industry and Trade, would no longer be able to attend the meeting scheduled to discuss the proposals put by the American Delegation. The meeting would now be attended by two staffers from the Ministry for the Development of the Russian Far East and Arctic. Dimitry smiled and informed the Americans that the senior staffers, Piotr Gansk and Saskia Temu would arrive in two hours. Dimitri smiled again and departed.

"Dimitri smiles a lot doesn't he," Ben Harper said. Harper was one of those people who spoke with his whole body, and he always had a lot to say. He was a big man. Jessica Haines, his trade partner, was a small, mousy woman who excelled in these trade meetings simply because no one took her seriously.

The four of them sat wondering where they had made their mistake. Pepworth and Tremaine did not say anything. They were junior delegates and were basically just on the delegation for the sake of experience. They waited for the pronouncements of Harper and Haines before they offered any of their own thoughts.

"We have pissed somebody off that's for sure," Haines said. "Do you think it was because we wouldn't discuss anything in our rooms, and we kept coming to this park to plan? They may have thought that was a bit insulting."

"Everybody assumes their rooms are bugged," Harper said. "Hell, even the Russians have meetings away from their rooms. This park is probably bugged as well."

Haines checked the agenda on her phone. "Well, we haven't changed anything." She flicked through a few pages on her phone. "The agenda is still the same. I don't understand why we have been downgraded to only getting ordinary staffers." She hit some keys on her phone. "I can't even find these people, Gansk and Temu. How senior can they be?"

"And the department?" Harper said. "What was it? Something about the Arctic?"

"The Ministry for the Development of the Russian Far East and Arctic," Billings read from his notes.

"Jesus. How downgraded can we get?" Harper said.

*

The meeting took place in a small but well-appointed room. The colours were all pastels, and the room was well lit and airy. The Russian Delegation stood and warmly welcomed the Americans before offering them coffee and pastries. They chatted and ate and made small jokes mainly about Britain. Finally, Piotr Gansk suggested that they begin their meeting proper and the six people sat.

"Your English is very good," Haines said.

"So is yours," Gansk replied to a ripple of laughter. "Our British friends would be proud of us both."

Haines and Harper exchanged a glance and Harper nodded.

"Before we begin negotiations, we have a slightly delicate question to ask." Haines was about to continue but Temu interrupted her.

"You wish to know why you are talking to a pair of lowly clerks from some obscure ministry."

"I would have put it more delicately than that," Haines said.

"I am sure you would have," Temu said. "And if we can raise also a delicate matter..."

"Of course," said Harper who felt they were moving very quickly for a trade meeting.

Gansk removed some papers from his satchel. He flicked through a few pages and then, satisfied, he placed a copy of a page in front of both Harper and Haines.

"We were wondering," Gansk began, "Would it be possible to remove the reference to Russia in the papers relating to your Roswell incident. The reasons for this request are:

One – The information is simply not true. We did not use children in experiments of either aircraft of genetics.

Two – We wouldn't send a spy plane over the airspace of the United States of America

Three – There is an implication that..." and here Temu leant over to whisper something to Gansk, "I am sorry. There is the *assertion* that Russian Airforce colluded with Nazi elements in said experimental aircraft." Gansk placed his paper back into its folder and sat awaiting a response from the Americans.

*

Harper held the bricklike phone while, Haines tried to block the wind blowing around revolution Square.

"Yes Director Davies," Harper said. "They want us to change the statement regarding the Roswell incident."

The phone made Davies sound like he was in a vacant hall. "Hell Harper, do you know how many times we have changed that story?"

"Well, they aren't going to go ahead with any of the trade deals unless we show some goodwill on this one Sir. I hate to raise it but you need to know that the President is very keen to get some strong links going with Russia and this is our best chance." Harper felt like he was shouting and trying to keep his voice from being recorded at the same time.

Davies sounded tired. "Yeah, I get it. Look, tell you what...We no doubt want to put some heat on someone, somewhere. Tell the Russians that we will say that the Roswell lights were merely us trialling some experimental weapons for use on our enemies in the Middle East. How does that sound?"

"And the bodies?" Haines whispered loudly to Harper. "Ask him about the bodies."

"What about the bodies that were photographed being removed from the umm experimental aircraft?"

"Oh Yeah, I forgot about them. Ok, let's go with crash test dummies. That's why they weren't full size humans."

2007

Wendell Wrantz opened the front door of the Centre For Extra Terrestrial Studies (CFETS) with a little difficulty. It had always stuck and for the one hundredth time he resolved to fix the door before he injured his shoulder.... Again. Wrantz was 66 years old, and he had already had major surgery on his left shoulder. He had also had both of his knees replaced and was currently wearing wrist bands that he hoped would relieve the pain caused by his carpel tunnel syndrome. He was thin because he did not eat much, but he was not fit, because he didn't exercise much either. The only thing he had going for him in a physical sense was his hair, which was thick, luxurious and which seemed to get darker with age and the application of colouring. The Director of the CFETS, Bruce Havers had already fired up the heater and had the kettle on for some coffee. Havers was also in his mid-60' s. He was grey, wiry and lean, and suffered from whatever illness he had last read about. Wrantz said "Hi" and settled into the committee room. He was followed by

Havers, and they sat on opposite sides of the table There were seats for seven in total, but it had been a long time since they had every seat taken for a committee meeting.

"How is the neuropathy?" Wrantz asked.

"Not bad," Havers said. "Got a feeling my arthritis is going to be playing up though."

"Have we got an agenda?" Wrantz asked.

Havers slid a piece of paper over to Wrantz and began to read from his own copy.

"One. We have to have a discussion about changing the name of the C.F.E.T.S or of maybe just dropping the F in the acronym."

"Again?" Wrantz asked plaintively. "We discuss this every damn meeting."

"Yeah, well you know how Lizzy is." Lizzy Jelane was the treasurer for the CFETS. She was 70 and it would be kinder to describe her as matronly than anything else. She arrived as Wrantz and Havers were discussing the agenda. They both said "Hi" to her and she said "Hi" back before settling into her usual place at the table.

"How is the neuropathy, Bruce?" Lizzy asked.

"Not bad, but I think my arthritis is going to kick in soon."

"If it isn't one thing, it' s another," Wendle said.

"The joys of getting old," Lizzy said.

"Beats the alternative," Havers said.

The three of them chuckled and then stopped chuckling when they thought of Gary Hayes who had chosen the alternative about six weeks previously, thereby reducing the CFETS to just three people in the process.

"Ok I think everyone is here," Havers said. He even looked around the small room as if to confirm this statement. "We don't have a lot to get through and you can see from the copy of the agenda in front of you..." He suddenly realised that Lizzy did not have a copy of the agenda. "Sorry Lizzy the copier ran out of paper. Can you two share?" Wrantz moved his copy closer to Lizzy so that she could follow along. "But I would like to point out that I do have an item that arrived too late to place on the agenda so I will be raising a point without notice. Now then, item one is the proposed name change for the CFETS. I'll hand over to Lizzy for this one."

"Thanks Bruce. I know Wendel here is opposed to this one, but I really feel we will get more traction in the media if we can shorten our name to the CETS. We can leave out the "for" bit cos no one puts those little words into their acronym. The C.F.E.T.S. is just too wordy."

"Well, I guess we open it up for discussion," Havers said.

Wrantz put his hand up and Havers nodded toward him.

"Look, I can see Lizzy's point about the acronym, but if we change it, we have to change all of the stationary. As Bruce here just pointed out, we don't have enough money to buy plain paper for the photocopier let alone design a whole new letterhead, so I think we need to put the name change on the back burner until we are a bit more flush with funds."

"In other words, never," Lizzy said.

"Now that isn't what Wendel said, Lizzy."

"Might as well be," Lizzy said. "Is that it? Is that the whole agenda?"

Bruce Havers seemed to be gathering himself together for a big moment. He shuffled some papers that were in front of him and adjusted his glasses.

"I do have another item to discuss." He withdrew a page from among the papers before him. "I have here a draft letter that I am proposing be sent to the Department of Homeland Security. It details our demands for the full disclosure of information relating to both the Roswell incident and the ongoing research being undertaken at Area 51. The letter also calls for the ongoing investigation of all visitations, abductions, interactions etc related to extra-terrestrial activity here in the United States and around the world. I have signed it on behalf of the executive body of the Center for Extra Terrestrial Studies. If approved, I intend to post it asap."

*

Department for Homeland Security – D Division
   Memo – All Staff
   As per the guidelines for all queries regarding the R file and Area 51 activities, we have reached the numerical point that instigates a change in policy. For newer staff, it was decided that as soon as we received 10,001 demands from various interest groups and individuals regarding our knowledge of the so-called Roswell Incident and Area 51, it would trigger a new explanation for the events. The winner of the sweep was J. Cooper from Accounts who drew the Center for Extra Terrestrial Studies or the CFETS. Well done, Jilly.
   Please note that from this moment onwards we will be attributing the phenomenon associated with Roswell to a highly unusual climatic event and ball lightening. It is felt that this cutting of ties to actual flying machines will be beneficial.
   2017
   The building was non-descript. It was on Highway 285 in the middle of Roswell, just near McDonalds. There were no signs on the building and there was very little in the way of foot traffic going in and out. There was, however, an amazing array of CCTV cameras and other surveillance equipment. Jeff Bezel pulled up right outside the building. Bezel had that weather beaten look that only comes from being, well, beaten by the weather. It was not a look that was going to be achieved in a tanning salon. Bezel was 60ish, around 6 footish and weighed a bit. In many ways he was as non-descript as the building he was surveying. He stomped up to the door of the

building and knocked. He waited for a minute and then knocked again. He turned and admired his truck. It was red, it was dusty, and it was weighed down at the back by a piece of otherworldly machinery. He turned around when he heard the door open.

"Yes?" A woman stood looking at Bezel through the security screen.

"Hi. My name is Jeff Bezel. I have a bit of machinery I want to show you."

The woman sighed dramatically. "We are not the local chapter of the UFO society. The UFO Museum is down the street and around the corner. Good day."

"I'm sorry Ma'am," Jeff said. "Everyone knows what this place is, and I don't need the Museum. I've seen enough plastic, fake supposed alien junk to last me a lifetime."

"Did you say your name was Bezel?"

"Yes Ma'am. Jeff Bezel. Mack was my grandad."

The woman looked up and down the street. She was almost birdlike in the way her head flicked from side to side, and this was accentuated by her short cropped red hair and bright eyes. She opened the door Jeff strolled into a smart office area.

"I'm sorry Mr. Bezel. We get a lot of umm…Interesting people coming here with… artifacts. I'm Marion Peck. How can I help you?"

"Well Miss Peck…"

"Marion, please."

"Marion. I was ploughing up a part of Grampa's land and I found something. It is in the back of my truck. Can't say I want it on my property, and I figured you people might want to have a look at it."

"I see. Is it heavy?"

"Yes Ma'am, it is."

"Can you bring it around the back?"

Marion followed Jeff as he made his way to the door. They both heard the excited voices before they reached it. As Jeff opened the door, he saw a crowd gathered around the back of his truck. Someone had thrown the tarp back and everyone was reaching in and trying to pry bits from the metal structure. There were even a few photographers from the local paper trying to get people to move away as they took shots. One of the people saw Jeff.

"Hey, it is you!" The man turned to the others. "I tol' you. I said it was Jeff Bezel's truck!"

And then the crowd left the truck and came rushing toward the door.

"Is that another UFO Mr. Bezel?" Where did you find it?" "Is it a part of the original?"

Finally, one man grabbed Jeff's hand and shook it excitedly.

"Mr. Bezel, I'm Jimmy Hever. I'm the new president of the Centre for Extra Terrestrial Studies or CETS. That's like SETS but with a "C". Can I get a picture with you?"

Marion finally yanked Jeff back into the building. She called out the name Hank and a burly man in his thirties walked into the reception area.

"Hank This is Jeff Bezel. His truck is outside. Can you drive it around back? There is a crowd around it." Hank simply nodded, accepted the keys from Jeff and went out the door.

"It's ok," Marion said. "Crowds tend to part for Hank."

Jeff heard his truck start up and drive away.

"So, is it?" Marion asked.

"Is it what?"

"Is it a part of the original?"

"I thought they only owned up to the original thing as being a weather balloon?"

Marion laughed. "Oh, that was long ago," she said. "I daresay the powers that be are not going to be happy about this new piece of evidence you have brought in. The current explanation is that the whole thing was down to a weird weather event and ball lightning. They will have to change it again now."

*

There were only four people present and none of them knew each other's name or any identifying details. One woman was talkative. One man was tall. The other woman was quiet, and the second man was far older than the other three people. They sat making small talk. Actually, it was extremely small talk as they all stuck to topics that just didn't matter. The weather got comprehensively covered. To everyone's considerable relief, General Meyers eventually entered the room.

"Good morning, ladies and gentlemen. Sorry to drag you all in on a Sunday, but that's the way it happens sometimes."

"We hear there has been another alien discovery," the talkative woman said.

"Incorrect," Meyers said. "There has been an addition to a previous discovery. A new part of the ship that was originally found on the Bezel farm."

"The Weather balloon?" the older man said.

"No. The next discovery. Same time, but this is a part of the actual craft that we took to Area 51."

"The one with the aliens?" the tall man said.

"Correct," Meyers said. "And sadly, the press and social media have got a hold of this one. The local media were alerted to the find in Roswell and it has just gone bananas since then."

"Viral," the talkative woman said. "It's gone viral."

"Whatever," Meyers said. "The upshot is, we have to come up with a new story."

"What is the story at the moment?" the older man asked.

Meyer referred to his notes. "Ah...Oh yes. Freak weather event coupled with ball lightning. Served us well as it got us right away from speculation about aliens and flying saucers."

"But the aliens and flying saucer stuff keeps cropping up anyway," the quiet woman said.

"Ah but only because the New Mexico government keeps leaking stories about aliens to maintain the tourist trade," the older man said.

"You can see on the list beside you, all of the explanations that we have used so far," Meyers said. "Now we aren't averse necessarily to reusing some or one of these, but I feel the time has come for a new, fresh approach."

"It sounds like you have an idea," the tall man said.

Meyer took some notes out of his briefcase. "It's a pretty rough idea...I'm thinking we could just tell the truth."

"The truth?"

"Yep, we just come out and say it. We found an alien spaceship. It had real aliens inside it. Sadly, we were unable to save them, but we did in fact perform autopsies on them. We can add that we have developed a lot of new technology based on our study of the ship. We can even say that aliens have been visiting us every so often for decades, but they don't seem to want to stop and chat."

The four people sat and thought about this for a moment.

"The truth," the quiet woman said.

The General nodded.

"What about the alien abductions? Are we going to come clean about that?"

"I don't see the need to mention those just yet," Meyers said. "I think the stuff about Roswell is enough to be going on with."

"Ok. Let's do it!" the old man said,

2027

Jimmy Hever sat in the air-conditioned comfort of the S.E.T.S. committee room. His secretary brought coffee and pastries in on a wheeled trolley.

"The others will be here in five minutes Mr. Hever."

"Thanks Kirsty," Jimmy said.

Jimmy checked the tech for the presentation and quickly read through his agenda. There was not too much to get through, but these meetings always seemed to get bogged down in details about peripheral details. Jimmy was keen to keep this meeting on track. The board of the SETS. began to arrive and soon they had a quorum. Jimmy waited until the scheduled start time of 11am and by that time an extra eight people had arrived. There were now twenty people in total.

"Good morning, everyone," Jimmy said. "I'm pleased to see everyone here and even more pleased that everyone is on time for once." There were some rueful smiles around the table; This was a favourite topic for Jimmy, and everyone expected it.

"Let's jump straight in with Item one on the agenda. Now this one is a perennial bugbear of some people here and we seem to discuss it every meeting."

Kenny Grantham raised his hand and began to talk before Jimmy, as chair, gave him the floor.

"It gets raised every meeting because spelling Center with an "S" so that it makes a nicer acronym is stupid."

"It gets us publicity," Maresy Killop said.

"It does," Kenny said. "But only because it is so stupid."

The debate went on for ten minutes until it finally ran out of steam, and it was agreed to form a subcommittee to determine whether the deliberate mis spelling of the word "center" was a plus or minus for the organisation. Jimmy then regained control of the meeting to discuss what was of far greater concern to him.

"Fellow committee members, back in 2017 when the Government released the news that they had found alien remains and technology in Roswell, they were rightly condemned for promulgating fake news." This pronouncement was greeted with a fairly muted chant of "Fake news. Fake news" before Jimmy quelled it with a raise of his hand. Since that time the Government has clearly decided that they can release any old news and get away with it. We have heard for instance about the so-called truth about the moon landings, JFK, Bigfoot, Area 51, John Lennon's death, the Depression, etcetera.

The government feels they can just put out anything they like.

Now, you all know me and I'm a realist if nothing else. Maybe a lot of what the government says and does can be explained away. But, and I want you to just work with me here for a moment...What if the Government really did find alien artifacts in the desert around Roswell way back then? What if it were all true?"

"You mean...When they said they found aliens...It wasn't fake news?"

"That's exactly what I mean," Jimmy said.

"And they only put the news out because they knew it would be discounted as fake news?"

Jimmy just nodded.

"Hell's bells they are a tricky bunch of bastards," Kenny Grantham said with passion. "They had me fooled."

"They had everyone fooled," Jimmy said.

Notes for Some of the People, Some of the Time.

I wrote this simply because I wanted to write a UFO story. I did a little bit of research so that various names and places would ring true, but obviously most of it is made up. I remember that there had been a few books about Roswell released just before I wrote this story, so I am assuming that the basic idea was fuelled by that fact. I think it is funny, but I may be the only one who thinks that. Time will tell I suppose.

I was glad I decided to break the story up into decades as that allowed me to write a 'short' short story for each decade. It also allowed me to use and re use characters. It is sort of like having a load of smaller episodes of an ongoing story. Like many of my stories, I had a lot of fun writing this. So much so that I mistrusted the story. By that I mean I wasn't sure if it was any good or not. I know I liked it but I am not so sure that my tastes are aligned with everybody else's. This fact may not bode well for the success of this collection of stories.

About 'So, you want to be a ....'

Way back in issue #11 of Aurealis, we decided to include a humorous piece at the back of the magazine as a bit of light relief. This idea developed into a series of articles. One such series of articles was "So, you want to be a...." which was simply an excuse to poke fun at various aspects of genre writing. Sometimes these pieces really hit the mark and other times not so much. Purists will be outraged to know that I have changed these a little. I have added where I thought of something funny to add, and subtracted where I thought it wasn't funny to begin with.

In the interest of protecting myself from undue criticism, I will just add that I do not consider myself an expert in any of these areas. It was all just a bit of fun.

So, you want to be a Fantasy Writer...

Writing fantasy can be a rewarding experience financially, spiritually and as a cure for insomnia. It's easy and it's fun!

Here is what you will need:

- A pen
- Lots of paper
- An extremely powerful and tolerant word processor
- A good imagination and/or a working knowledge of copyright laws.

Fantasy can be broken down into a number of sub-genres, and it would be wise for the budding Fantasy writer (or Bandwagoner as they are known in the trade) to familiarize himself, or herself with all of them so as to be able to take full advantage of market fluctuations and mood swings.

Straight Fantasy - Possibly not what you are thinking. If it is some sort of sexual content, you are looking for you need to refer to the entry on Dark Fantasy. Anyway, Straight Fantasy is the biggest sub-genre. It contains elements of all of the other sub genres and is the best-selling sub-genre. It also has been around for a long time. It generally involves a quest, some sort of magical item that was once lost, an evil lord, some good lords, a council of some description, vast heroic armies led by great heroic kings and of course, a young person who looks after the goats. It doesn't have to be a goatherd, of course. You could use a shepherd, but I would advise against going with someone who tends rabbits, or who raises Alpacas. They just aren't Fantasy material.

High Fantasy - Exactly the same as Straight Fantasy, except it has more elves in it.

Dark Fantasy - This is a tricky one. Dark Fantasy does not really need kings and magic etc as long as there is plenty of blood, violence and sex or, at the very least the *promise* of lots of blood, violence and sex. If you include any of the elements of Straight Fantasy you will have to increase the amount of blood, violence and sex proportionately. For every magic ring, amulet or sword, you will need to include a sex scene. All wizards, lords and virtuous Kings will need to be offset with some dungeons, torture and some sort of S&M. Should you feel compelled to include the goatherd, I can only suggest you read *American Psycho* and see if you can't incorporate parts of that into the narrative.

Sword and Sorcery - Knights and Wizards and mythical beasts. More violent than *Straight* and *High*, but not as violent as *Dark*. You will need some bulging biceps on the cover on one of these.

Magical Realism - No one really knows what this is, so if you have written a book that does not include any of the above, but which still seems a little left of centre, call it *Magical Realism*. But remember, it must be dull enough to be mistaken for something that seems to have literary merit.

Cozy Fantasy - The new kid on the block. Safe, non-threatening and marginally funny. Often involves characters with violent pasts who have forsaken that part of their lives and gone to retire in a small village in Hobbit...sorry, in some rural area. Often involves a lot of food and beverages,

Let's take a look at some of the other aspects of the fantasy genre.

Names - An often overlooked area in Fantasy is the naming of characters. Some writers just do not take the time to invent decent names for their characters or places, but it is so easy! The best way to go about this is to take a word, (any word but the longer the better) mix up the letters, and then pick out some names. Easy! The trick is giving the right names to the right characters.

Here is an example; Say we choose the word MARKET. We immediately have a name. Can you spot it? ARKET. It could be the name of the goatherd, but it could also be the name of his village. It could even be the name of his simple but virtuous smithy father, who is a former soldier with a secret past.

Let's see what else we have: KARM - A heroine who is good with horses; TEKRAM (always use the word backwards just in case it "works") Arket's rival goatherd, not necessarily evil, but just easily led; KRAM - a soldier; MAKET - another village; and KRET - another soldier (soldiers account for an awful lot of names in Fantasy).

"But these are all good names," you say. "What about all the Evil Wizards, Dark Overlords and the like?" Simple. You just add a "G" to your letters, or, if you want someone really evil, you add a "Z". You can add both if you really want to hammer home the point. A "G" added to the letters in the word MARKET gives us: GRARK - An evil soldier or perhaps a mythical beast; TEKGAR - An evil wizard, or maybe a city; and RAGTEK - Possibly another evil soldier.

Now if we also add a "Z" we get: ZEMKAR - The evil one! Even more evil? ZGEMKAR! A subtle but important difference.

The only limit is your imagination. If you happen to have trouble spelling, that could be seen as a bonus. Remember though that you must use the right name for the right character. KARM for instance, just does not work as the name for an evil soldier. GRARK the horse loving heroine? No way!

Terminology - It is all in *how* you say things. "Arket smote the very living rock itself with his exceptionally broad bladed weapon whose shaft was honed from the wood of the rare and powerful *jhinar* tree, and whose handle was cunningly wrought from precious metal hitherto unseen; yet still the rock would not yield," does not necessarily mean, "Arket did a bit of gardening with his shovel, and the ground was really hard." But just while we are here looking at this bit of fine writing...

Rock is never just rock. It is either, *The* living rock, or The Very living rock, itself. This is related to the fact that it is never just "cloudy" and "windy" in fantasy stories. If you want to get across the fact that it is cloudy and windy, you have clouds "scudding" across the sky. Fantasy is the only place where clouds "scud".

Just to finish off, here are some "Golden Rules:

- Fantasy comes in trilogies or more. Stephen Donaldson once completed a fantasy in two parts, but he is a Master.

- Get your cover art right! Lurid and garish for *Sword and Sorcery* and *Dark Fantasy*, subtle for *Straight* and *High*, obscure for Magical Realism. Oh, and cartoonish for *Cozy*.

- Maps. Many fantasy writers write enormous fantasy books simply so that they get to draw maps. I think many would prefer to just do the maps and not worry about the actual books, but the market does not see it that way. Anyway, don't forget to have plenty of squiggly bits in your maps. And make sure you have lots of maps.

- If in doubt, pad it out. There is a reason fantasy books are nearly all doorstops.

- Rings, swords, crowns and staffs are all acceptable magical items. Cardboard boxes, mops and juice extractors are not.

So, you want to be a Science Fiction Writer...

If you are interested in writing science fiction, the first thing you need to decide is what you are going to call it. The argument surrounding "science fiction" as a name for the genre has been going on for decades and is still unresolved. Here are your options:

Science fiction - sort of old fashioned and with far too many syllables for today's audiences.

Sci Fi - Gets marks for number of syllables, but really is only used when you want to upset large parts of the fan community.

SF - Modern looking, catchy and really scores on the syllable score, but still does not satisfy many purists.

Speculative Fiction - The inoffensive catch all name that tries to please everyone. Sounds vaguely "literary" so it scores well on that front.

Now your next decision is which sub-genre are you going to focus on? Honestly, there are more choices here than you can poke a light sabre at. Here are just a few: time travel, alternate worlds, space opera, aliens, cyberpunk, robots, lost worlds, lost races, lost manuscripts. I will have to prune the options somewhat, but let's see if we can tempt you with some more detailed descriptions:

Space Opera - This one has always been popular. If your story is set in space, the chances are your story is Space Opera. Unless it features some other aspect of science fiction in as much or greater detail than the actual space bit. For instance, if your story tells the tale of a spaceship cruising in outer space. It is space opera. If your crew meets aliens, it is still space opera, unless the aliens then go on to invade the earth when it becomes an Aliens story. Similarly, if your crew return to earth and everything has changed, then it becomes an alternate earth story, unless the reason that everything has changed is because of time dilation, and your crew haven't aged much whilst their own children are now elderly citizens. Then it is a Time Travel story.

Anyway, as the late great Douglas Adams once pointed out, space is big. It has to be in order to accommodate all of the empires, foundations, civilisations and regimes that people are keen to boldly go to. It is a sobering thought that, if all of these civilisations and empires etc. were real, you would have more arguments, and wars and bitter disputes than you could reasonably expect at a major SF convention. Oh ok, it probably wouldn't be that bad, but you get the idea.

Space Opera is relatively easy to write because all you have to do is take any empire that has been well researched and written about, e.g. The Roman Empire, the Nazi empire, the McDonald's empire, and bung it into space. Now the big problem is getting your characters from A to B, given the fact that A and B are light years apart and in the real world would take longer to traverse than the M1 in peak hour traffic. What you need is some sort of drive for your spaceships. It doesn't matter what it is, I mean, you don't have to actually invent the thing. You don't even need to explain it in much detail. You just need to give it a good name: The Ferguson Drive, or the Prentice Engine, or the Nguyen Effect. The reader does not need to know how the drive works, just that it does. Your characters do not need to know either.

Speaking of characters, if you are a truly gifted writer, if you can write brilliant dialogue and create believable characters, then maybe this category isn't for you. Space Opera calls for characters so wooden they should have names like Ben Teak and Mahogany Pine. The idea is the thing!

Social SF - This s a bit like *1984* only set in the future. Obviously when George Orwell wrote *1984* it *was* set in the future, and this highlights a problem with this category. It has a use by date. Don't go making any startling claims that will be proved wrong while you are still around. By all means use this sub-genre to express some Marxist angst or whatever you want to get off your chest, but don't get too preachy. This category also allows you to work in some of the other sub genres and Time Travel is obviously suited to this one as you can show just how rotten some social problem is going to become given a substantial lapse of time. If you are thinking of using this sub-genre to espouse your thoughts on Climate change, I would get a move on if I were you.... Especially if you live in a low-lying area.

Time Travel - You need to be careful with Time Travel as it has a tendency to take over the plot. The last thing you want when you are juggling a load of different plot lines is some character constantly appearing and worrying about the fact that he has just killed his own great grandfather. Time Travel is very, very tricky and is probably best left to the experts like car mechanics and people who frequent doctor's waiting rooms. Think about it.

Aliens - Another really popular sub-genre. The big problem here is that no matter how original your story is, it isn't.

Utopias and Dystopias - Utopias are imagined societies where everything is well ordered and everybody is happy, and Dystopias are not.

Time Travel - Very, very tricky.

Robots - Isaac Asimov pretty much cornered the market on robots. He came up with the three laws of robotics and wrote a heap of stories about them. You could try and come up with your own three laws and see if you can make a name for yourself:

1. Have you tried turning it on and off again? (Sorry)
2. Read the bloody instructions!
3. If problems persist, see your dealer.

Time Travel - Very, very tricky... hang on a second!

Some golden rules.

- If you are thinking of publishing in America, don't forget to include your middle initial. Otherwise whack a Jnr at the end of your name.

- No matter what your story is about, stick a picture of a spaceship on the cover. Preferably one with yellow and black stripes.

- Remember to include a good bio of yourself. You are creating a work of fiction so you might as well start here.

- It is always nice to have an award or two after your name. The fact that they are cricket trophies need not be mentioned. For instance, I would put, "Stephen Higgins - Winner of an HCA award!" (Horsham Cricket Association)

So, You Want to be a Horror Writer...

Well, these days who doesn't? Everywhere you look there are new anthologies, new novels and new authors. Let's take a look at what makes a horror writer, and you can see if you have what it takes.

1. Do you have to have a bloodthirsty disposition? Not necessarily, but it helps.

2. Do you need some basic knowledge of anatomy? Not necessarily, but it helps.

3. Do you need a talent for writing? Not necessarily, but the first two points are still fresh in my mind so perhaps we should move on.

Horror writing might have been invented by the Goths, or the Visigoths who were a race of people much interested in violence, architecture and I guess literature. Hence the terms *Gothic Horror* and *Gothic Architecture*. The average Goth's propensity to engage in violent acts, coupled with a love of retelling the day's exploits to their friends inevitably led to the invention of what we know today as *Horror* writing. It also led to some ugly architecture.

The term "Gothic" came to refer to a style of writing rather than an actual group of people, or a period in time. *Gothic Horror* got a bit bogged down in the 19th Century, and its icons were employed fairly arbitrarily in an attempt to secure sales. You only had to mention fog covered moors and you were stuck with the Gothic label, even if you were only writing a gardening book. This was in fact how *Gothic Romance* came into being, as well as the lesser-known sub genres *Gothic Western, Gothic Crime* and *Gothic Historical Fiction.* An interesting point arose from *Gothic Historical Fiction.* It proved to be quite a popular genre and spun off a few sub genres of its own. One of these dealt exclusively with the Gothic age and was tagged *Gothic Gothic.* Another sub-genre was *Gothic Light Romantic Comedy,* but it never really caught on.

This plethora of Gothic styles led to an oversupply in the market and the publishers of horror writing decided to lift the image of their product by renaming it and relaunching it. They wanted a name that sounded respectable, but which still alluded to the horrific nature of the genre. They wanted a literary flavour that still appealed to the homicidal maniac. *Gothic Horror* had been fine, but was now overused and *Horror* by itself was too restricting. Thus, *Scary Writing* was spawned. (Nothing is ever "born" in *Horror*. It is all spawned or exhumed.) This was followed rapidly by *Weird Stuff*, *Bloody Books* and *Spine Tingling, Mind numbingly Fearful and Apprehensive Writing* (An American appellation) and finally, *Dark Fantasy*. As is the way of these things, *Dark Fantasy* went off on a bit of a tangent and the publishers went back to plain old *Horror*.

The material that has been critically acclaimed as work of a high literary standard emanating from the *Horror* genre is impressive. It was written in 1818 by Mary Shelley, and it was called *Frankenstein or The Modern Prometheus*. Very soon, every publisher and their canine friend were publishing books under the catch all imprint of *Horror*, regardless of the books' contents. It is a little-known fact that Poe's *The Fall of the House of Usher* was originally a treatise on architectural decay, first published in a small magazine called *The Brickies Mate*.

This practice continues today. The novels of Stephen King are completely re-written and hold none of the grandeur of his original intent. Salem's Lot, for instance, was originally all about the owner of a car yard where the young Stephen King worked during school vacations as a car detailer. (See also The Shining)

The budding, or emerging, horror writer should now know what it takes to be a success in the field: an unscrupulous publisher. It would help to include some elements of classic horror in your story. I can only direct you to a lovely little book called The New Gothic (What else?) edited by Patrick McGrath and Bradford Morrow. In the introduction to this anthology, the editors point out that good Horror writing contains a lot of 'furniture'. Now it may be that I have grasped the wrong end of the stick here, but I think it would be wise for the beginner to make sure they have a few coffee tables and sofas strewn about the story.

So, you want to be a Book Reviewer...

Really? Are you sure? Do the important people in your life know about this? Oh, all right then. You really do want to be a book reviewer. It would be ok to say no. No-one would judge you or anything. Right. Fine. Don't say I didn't warn you.

Being a book reviewer isn't all beer and skittles. In fact, there are hardly any skittles involved at all. Beer, yes. Skittles, no. Unless of course you are reviewing a book about skittles, in which case the subject may come up, but it is still no certainty.

There is one golden rule to be followed when setting out to be a book reviewer. This one simple, basic rule is often ignored by beginners as well as by some of our more noted reviewers. I cannot over emphasise the importance of following this rule: Never, I repeat never, read the book you are about to review. Flick through it certainly. Pick out a few quotes, by all means, but do not read it. Many a promising review has come to grief simply because the reviewer knows too much about the book.

"So, what do I write about?" You might ask. Well, the book has a cover doesn't it? Some struggling artist put a lot of time and effort (or no time and effort depending on the cover) into that cover and you want to just ignore it? How many pages are there? Today's readers want value for money. Is the paper nice to the touch? Is it well bound? If it is a digital book, are the pixels all in the right place? Are there any pictures or maps?

And you thought there was nothing to write about!

There will come a time when you will be asked to review what is known in the trade as a "toughie". It will be an average sized book, average weight, with ok sort of paper or pixels. You know the type of thing. Even the cover art is nothing to write a book about. Now is the time to glance through the book. Skim read it a little. Read the blurbs on the back to see what it is about. That is what they are there for. And then you write your review bearing in mind the following:

You will have noticed a lot of terms and phrases that keep cropping up in reviews. Learn them. If you want to succeed in this caper you will have to use them. They form a code that all readers come to know, and the reader will expect you to use them. I have listed the main ones here, as well as their translations.

A joy to read - The reviewer is being paid cash.

A good read - Not a lot of spelling mistakes.

A very good read - Only one or two spelling mistakes

An excellent read - No spelling mistakes that I could see.

Powerful - Long.

Emotionally charged - It's got sex in it.

Sensuous - It's got sex in it.

The interactions between the diverse, compelling characters are one of the strengths of this book. I found myself actually caring about the people - It's got sex in it.

Dazzling - It has a shiny cover.

A triumph - One assumes that the author at least must have read it all the way through and that is an achievement.

A work of immense intelligence - See *An excellent read*.

Informative - The pages are numbered.

Well structured - The pages are numbered consecutively.

Challenging - The pages are not numbered consecutively.

Impressive - Lots of pages

Interesting, well drawn characters - It has people in it.

A rich and detailed sense of place - It is set somewhere

Evocative, thematic, inter-textual, postmodern, interpretative, reflective, intuitive - It has no plot.

Exotic, luscious, sublime, rolling cadence, pendant terminating clause, plangent - The author owns a thesaurus.

A classic work that showcases all of the talents of (author) - It was written by (author)

Each successive novel by (author) is distinctly better than the last - This is the author's first book.

The best book I have read - This is my first.

A return to form - The author did manage one good book, but this is more true to style.

A rollicking, roller coaster ride - It induces nausea.

The best book this year - It is January.

In conclusion, a word of warning: for some reason, authors dislike receiving bad reviews or 'uninformed crap' as they call them. If you write a negative review you can expect to hear from the author, the publisher, the authors friends and workmates, their fans, family and in extreme cases, their dogs. Do not be daunted. You are providing a service to the reader. If you don't like a book, just call it a work of relevance, and cop the flak.

About 'Sacred Cows'

I'm not really sure where the idea for this series of articles came from. I probably just thought about lampooning a classic SF text and the idea grew from there. The conceit behind these pieces is that they are written as if the book was a new release, thereby negating all of the influence that they might have had on the genre. It also means that they are sometimes compared with texts which, in reality, owed a lot to the subject of the piece. If that makes sense.

I remember that I was a little fearful that I would get someone who did not realise that it was a bit of fun and that they would think I really believed that these classic works were new releases. To tell the truth, I am still a bit worried that someone will read these pieces in this book and that they will point out that I am an idiot for thinking they are new works.

So, just to restate... These pieces were obviously not meant to be taken seriously. They are "Just a bit of fun." They were of course, written from a place of love and respect. Honest.

1984

By George Orwell

This new novel by English writer George Orwell sees him going in a new direction: backwards. *1984* is ostensibly set in the future, so, unless I have completely misread the book, it is set in an alternate past. Or it might be set in an alternate future's past. Or it could just be an alternate reality with a dodgy calendar. For quite some time I was worried that the whole thing may have been the victim of a prodigious typographical error, and it was supposed to be *2084*, or *2184*.

It is 1984.... we'll just take that as read for the moment, and the world is dominated by three powers, which is a novel twist because usually it is just two powers and a rag-tag collection of victims. Anyway, the action takes place in Oceania, which is like England, but not quite as grim. The country is ruled by The Party and that is about as far as accurate nomenclature goes in this novel. The Ministry of Love is into fear and hate, the Ministry of Peace presides over a never-ending war, and the Ministry of Truth deals with propaganda. You just can't get good proofreaders these days. I am beginning to think the title IS a typo.

Our hero is Winston Smith, and Arnold Schwarzenegger he ain't. A pity really because I could just see Arnie kicking ass if they ever do a movie of it. Obviously, they'd have to change a few things, like the plot, and the subplot, and the themes, and the artistic integrity, but that hasn't stopped them in the past! Anyway, our hero lives in a dilapidated apartment, and he works as a public servant in a thankless job. He participates in Hate Week, and he lusts after the girls in their Anti Sex League sashes. Someone told me that this bit is meant to be satirical, but I couldn't find any jokes in it. It is all pretty harrowing stuff to be honest.

It transpires that our hero has a bit of a conscience, and he is a tad concerned about the fact that the country that Oceania is at war with keeps changing. As a matter of fact, a lot of the past keeps changing as well. Now don't start thinking that we are off into time travel here because it is really about how the dominant ideology is able to control everything, even history, and this all fits in a major theme about ethics. Our hero then decides to fight this all-pervading evil by renting a room and having it off with his girlfriend. That'll show 'em! Anyway, this is probably the ethical bit. The evil government as personified by "Big Brother" (talk about clichés!) are onto Winston's cunning plan and they spy on the couple with a large video screen. Winston, realising the type of people he is up against, dobs in his girlfriend. Then they let him go.

It is a complex plot I know, but there are a few other things going on in the novel. Orwell actually invents a new language, for instance, called 'Newspeak'. This is how it works: if something is "good", it is called "good". If it is not "good", then, no, it is not called "bad". An easy mistake to make but bear with me - if a thing is not good, it is "ungood". Now, if this supposed thing were really, really bad, it would be called "doubleplusungood". I think maybe Mr Orwell may have invented "Newspeak" in the hope of covering up proofreading errors. "Newspeak" also contains the word "doublethink" which means "the power of holding two contradictory beliefs in one's mind simultaneously and accepting both of them." So, it is all about politics as well. This all demonstrates a pretty good imagination and ability with words...Well some of them anyway, which raises an interesting point.

I can't help thinking that Mr Orwell would have had a real winner on his hands if only he did something a little more imaginative with the names of his characters. Perhaps Winston Smith could be something like, maybe, James Luger, or Hunter McRae. He needs a more heroic name. Something with a bit of oomph. And Big Brother could be something like Zgemmkar. There is another evil figure in the book: O'Brien. Yeah, I know - Yawn. He could be called something like Skarrik. No first name. At least Orwell got that right. Just Skarrik. It has to be something like that, because, at first, you don't know that O'Brien is a bad guy. I hope I'm not giving too much of the plot away here.

Anyway, 1984 is a good read, although a little dated, and it gets a doubleplusgood rating from me.

Foundation
By Isaac Asimov

Here is a slim little volume that I found intriguing. Isaac Asimov is a little-known American author. Let me state here that his lack of popularity stems not from a lack of talent, but rather is due to the author's pathological self-effacement. He is, apparently, shy to a fault. Add to this his woefully meagre output and you begin to see why the name Asimov is not a little more prominent on the bookshelves. Hopefully *Foundation* will change all of that.

Foundation deals with the minutiae of human existence. It dissects and analyses every nuance of the human condition through an intimate portrayal of a close community spread across a million planets. It is like Jane Austen on an intergalactic scale.

The actual story deals with the efforts of Hari Seldon, a psychohistorian (aren't they all? Sorry ...) to limit the period of barbarism that will follow the fall of the current ruling Empire. The Empire is in a period of decline, you see, and it is about to fall. I don't know where Asimov got the inspiration for this novel plot line, but it's a corker. Actually, a better title for the book would be *The Decline and Fall of the* ... oh, hang on ... Anyway, Hari, the main character, dies. Now this would have presented a bit of a problem to a lesser writer, but the whole point of the story is that Hari knows what is going to happen next. This is what is so impressive about psychohistorians, they can predict the future. Not an individual's future, but that of a whole society. Before you get carried away with notions of entire civilisations going out to meet tall dark strangers and travelling overseas, I'd better point out that what is predicted are the trends a civilisation will follow.

These universal trends are as follows: Decline, Fall and then the building up of a Replacement. Given that the Decline is already well in place and the Fall is imminent, the astute reader might pick up a tiny flaw in the book. But that would be mere hair splitting. Okay, The Decline and Fall trends are a tad easy for Hari to predict, but he does get them in the right order. He could easily have said that there will be a Fall followed by a Decline. I will admit that he does cheat a little with the Replacement trend as well, because he actually sets up the Replacement for the Empire before the old Empire actually falls. I think this is called "betting on a sure thing".

The stylistic approach of the novel is worth commenting on because it is actually a series of short stories. Now, a lot of people heap abuse upon the short story writer — novelists mainly, but also a few essayists who feel threatened. Novelists claim that short stories are easy to write and are not worthy of publication, but the short story does have its own unique charms. They are short, and they are easy to read, and they pretty well form their own chapters, and lots of other attributes too numerous to mention here. And, contrary to popular opinion, they are *not* easy to write. Each short story has a beginning, a middle, and an end. I mention this because a lot of writers get them in the wrong order. But not Asimov. Here is a true master of the short story form. Not only has he written a series of short stories, each with its own beginning, middle and end, *in the right order*, but he has them put them one after the other and still got them in the right order! I guess that's psychohistory at work.

All in all, this book is a winner: well-rounded characters, beautifully realised settings, and, thanks to the short stories, more climaxes than you can poke a stick at. It even has a nice picture of a spaceship with red stripes on the cover. Nothing whatsoever to do with the story, but it always works as far as I'm concerned. My only hope is that Asimov will get on with some serious writing. And I am talking quantity here rather than quality. I feel he needs to increase his output and, unless I'm very much mistaken, I think there might be room for a sequel to *Foundation*.

The Lord of the Rings
By
J.R.R. Tolkien

Here is a novel that will really get the juices flowing for any fans of fantasy out there. This novel has a bit of a pedigree, and the discerning reader should note that this does not mean it's a bit of a dog. The Lord of the Rings has a debt to pay to other fantasy novels. National Budget deficits spring readily to mind when I think of that debt, but it does have some features that set it apart from the run of the mill fantasy novel. It is quite good for a start. Well-written, thoughtful. But for all that it is still a fantasy novel and therefore should be avoided by all those with a decent grounding in reality, and knowledge of the truth about fairies, pixies and the like.

Mr. Tolkien seems to have read and taken on board my little guide to writing fantasy (Aurealis #11). The book comes in three parts, always a sign of quality fantasy writing. There is a good council, bent on maintaining all that is decent. There are various bad guys and things called Hobbits that sound like a cross between the little guy on Fantasy Island and a rabbit. Mr. Tolkien did lose some marks here. What's wrong with good old shepherds or lowly-but-virtuous kitchen hands?

A few more points were lost with the naming of characters. The chief evil guy does not have a name starting with Z. He is called Sauron, which is sort of okay, but why not Zauron? It just looks more evil.

The plot is threadbare, but then it is fantasy and involves a bunch of Hobbits (Frodo and Bilbo Baggins — good names, Tolk!) finding and then trying to destroy a ring. What is it about fantasy writers and rings? Anyway, this special, magic mysterious ring allows the wearer to become invisible. Yeah, I know. Pretty intriguing concept isn't it. Anyway, they are helped in their quest by Gandalf the wizard, who is adept at fireworks. If you want a decent Catherine wheel, he's your man. Gandalf joins the halfwits — sorry halflings — on their perilous journey to the Crack of Doom, which is like a Warner Bros Movie World theme ride for manic depressives. They are accompanied by an irritating elf, a dwarf who was rejected for the part of Grumpy (overqualified), some more Hobbits, who, despite the absence of female Hobbits, seem to breed like rabbits, a glorified Park Ranger who turns out to be a king of some place, and a man, and, oh, another Hobbit.

There are sundry other stock fantasy characters, such as talking trees and orcs. Orcs are just goblins with attitude. The tokens that get collected by the fellowship, and there are always tokens to be collected in fantasy novels, include, apart from the magic ring, magic wood, magic crystal balls and a magic sword that was once broken but is now repaired and it can be used to kill people by pointing it at them and then stabbing them. Not very magic really when you think about it. The is also some magic dirt, and when you plant seeds in it, they grow. I think Tolkien's got a bit of work to do on his icons. There has been some talk around the fantasy traps (You know the sort of places I mean, wholistic coffee shops with stone ground coffee and free-range honey cakes) that Tolkien has ripped off a few ideas from Stephen Donaldson. Where Dono has woodhelvin, Tolks has elves. Stonedowners versus dwarfs, Giants and ents. There is possibly some truth in this but ... really. It is only fantasy. There is one aspect where Tolkien could take a leaf out of Donaldson's book, and some would argue that he's taken the twig, branch, trunk and roots anyway, and this is the area of sex. There isn't a scrap of it in Lord of the Rings.

There is not an awful lot more I can say about the Ring Trilogy, as it is bound to be called. It has nice castles, some good countryside scenes, lots of maps so all those map fans won't be disappointed. All in all, it's a fairly good book. I just can't see it setting the world on fire sales wise. Maybe with the second trilogy in the series. There is bound to be one.

The War of the Worlds
By
H.G. Wells

Well, I've heard of `retro" but this takes the cake. This novel is merely a thinly disguised re-write of some great movies of the same name. Oh sure Mr. Wells tries to hide this fact by setting it in Victorian England but come on...Actually there was a tv version set in Victorian England as well. Oh well, I guess we should expect a lot more of this sort of thing. I should also point out that fans of Independence Day will also experience a sense of déjà vu whilst reading this novel. I'm sure Mr. Wells will argue that his work is a homage to the great invasion movies, but there is a fine line between homage and cashing in.

Here's the plot; Martians (Yes Martians!) invade. They kill a lot of people. There is no way to stop them. They all get the flu and die. There are a few other sub plots - A philosophical gunner goes on and on about humans forming a new utopian society under the ground. He gets on the nerves of other characters and the reader. There is a vicar who tries to use the power of religion to defeat the Martians. He gets zapped, thereby demonstrating that a bible is no match against a heat ray. Didn't this fool of a man realise that God is on the side of the Americans? And that there are no Americans in this story? And why a heat ray? Why does alien technology have to be based on Victorian technology? Mind you, given the state of the Martians home they do seem to have given their heat ray a thorough testing.

There are some nice touches in the novel. Victorian England is lovingly constructed...Until it gets deconstructed by the Martians. There is a small love interest, although not as passionate and intense as that portrayed in the film. The actual Martians themselves are ok...Sort of like giant squid. Now what Mr. Wells could have done was to have some sort of hero (There are none in novel as it stands) and he or she could have captured a Martian flying...Sorry, walking machine and turned the heat ray on the Martians, thereby destroying their invasion plans and introducing calamari to Victorian England. Given the right treatment that could work.

Dune
By
Frank Herbert

Dune is that rare thing - a book that is what it says it is. If you are interested in sand, then this is the book for you. Much of the praise that has been lavished on *Dune* stems from the fact that Frank Herbert has created a plausible, believable world. It has even been stated that one of the strongest characters in the novel is the setting itself. However, given that the place is all sand, is this such an accomplishment?

Well yes and no. Ok the world of *Dune* is all sand. There is no getting around that. Oh yes there are a few rocks as well, but basically, sand. But it is well realised sand. It is plausible sand. There are other elements in the story. There are people. And worms. Big worms. They are called sandworms not inappropriately, and they perform a host of functions within the novel.

Let's just set the scene:

Dune, or Arrakis as it is known, is a very dry world. Remember when you got invited to a 'dry' wedding party and you thought "great, they can control the weather. No rain." Well, you would be just as wrong here if you were imagining a world where it doesn't rain much. This is a really, really dry world. When you die, they extract all of the water from your body, so it doesn't go to waste. I mean, full marks for conservation, zero for taste. And yes, it is used for drinking water. One wonders about the choice in restaurants: "Would you like still or sparkling? Or not from a corpse?" Anyway, it is really dry. With, as previously mentioned, lots of sand. The sand contains spice. As it would I suppose. Now this spice is special as it allows certain creatures to navigate spaceships through all of the curly bits in space.

It is therefore valuable as people have to travel through space to get away from dud planets with nothing on them but spicy sand and bloody big worms. This fact gives *Dune* its dramatic emphasis and provides Herbert with the MacGuffin of the story: Political intrigue. Herbert knew that sand alone would not an epic make so he put in a whole load of stuff about politics, religious mumbo jumbo and worm farming, and he came up with a winner.

The plot revolves around the adventures of Paul Atreides, the son of the man lumbered with Arrakis as a base, and how the young Paul survives attempts on his life by rival spice pushers and becomes a God figure. In this regard it is not unlike *The Godfather,* or some other mafia inspired story. If you can imagine a mixture of *The Godfather*, *Lawrence of Arabia* and *Beach Party a go go,* you can begin to get a feel for the thing.

Anyway, Paul Atreides is viewed by the locals as some sort of pre-ordained messiah and he promptly organises the huddled masses into a ruthless band of cut throat killers who worship the ground he walks on, even if it does keep moving beneath him. Now, this bit might be a metaphor. Paul is on shaky ground...The sand shifts beneath his feet... But I might be wrong. So, Paul's dad gets killed and his mum gets all involved with this bunch of women who sort of reminded me of the three witches in *Macbeth* so you can add that in as well. And put in *Richard the Third* as well.

So, what have we got? *Dune* is a combination of Mafia movies, New Age religions, Beach parties, *Lawrence of Arabia* a couple of Shakespearian plays, plus Space Opera and cults.... And of course, worms. At this stage of the proceedings, I should probably disabuse you of the notion of worms as soft, squidgy things that lie about in compost bins. These worms are huge and have teeth. In order to adequately get the terror inducing vibe of these things, you need to concentrate on the teeth.

The book was made into a film a few decades ago, and again more successfully recently. If you want to learn more about the world of *Dune,* you should certainly see the films. Or, and I do advise caution here, you could read some of the many sequels, or prequels...or spin offs. There are a great many of them.

Acknowledgements

Many thanks to Kathy for everything.

Thank you to everyone at Aurealis magazine for their help over the years.

Special thanks to Dirk Strasser and Michael Pryor who have given me tons of writing advice. This advice was generally delivered during our 'business' meetings which are actually just an excuse to talk about writing, movies and football. They are the only meetings I have ever really looked forward to attending.

Over the past few years I have made contact with a few people in the Australian SF writing scene, and I am always pleased and amazed at how welcoming they are, and how willing they are to provide assistance and advice.

I would also like to thank all of the writers whose work has given me great pleasure over the years, and whose stories have influenced and inspired me.

Story acknowledgements

'Water' first appeared in *Aurealis* #6 - 1991

    'Vignette' first appeared in *Aurealis* #2 - 1990

    'The Waiting Tree' first appeared in *Aurealis* #22 - 1998

    'Universe®' first appeared in *Aurealis* #25/26 - 2000

    'Forest/Tree' first appeared in *Aurealis* #100 - 2017

    'Cradle' first appeared in Aurealis #126 - 2019

Articles

'So, you want to be a Fantasy Writer...' first appeared in *Aurealis* #11 - 1993

    'So you want to be an SF Writer...' first appeared in *Aurealis* #12 - 1993

    'So you want to be a Horror Writer...' first appeared in *Aurealis* #13 - 1994

    'So you want to be a Book Reviewer...' first appeared in *Aurealis* #14 - 1994

    'SF's Sacred Cows: 1984' first appeared in *Aurealis* #16 - 1995

    'SF's Sacred Cows: Foundation' first appeared in *Aurealis* #17 - 1996

    'SF's Sacred Cows: The Lord of the Rings' first appeared in *Aurealis* #18 - 1996

    'SF's Sacred Cows: The War of the Worlds' first appeared in *Aurealis* #19 - 1997

    'SF's Sacred Cows: Dune' first appeared in *Aurealis* #20/21 1998

About the Author

Stephen Higgins has co-edited Aurealis with Dirk Strasser and Michael Pryor for decades. He also Co-hosts the Apocryphal Australia podcast, records and releases instrumental music, cooks, gardens and is into photography. He lives in rural Victoria, Australia. You can read Aurealis wherever you get your books. You can listen to Apocryphal Australia wherever you get your podcasts. You can listen to Stephen's music wherever you stream your music. Do you see how easy I am making all of this for you?

www.ingramcontent.com/pod-product-compliance
Lightning Source LLC
Chambersburg PA
CBHW052029020726
47501CB00004B/1321